Praise For The

A Straw Man

Brianna—
Time is a gift...
Use it wisely!

[signature]

A Straw Man

AMALIE JAHN

BERMLORD PUBLICATIONS

www.bermlord.weebly.com

Library of Congress Control Number: 9780991071326
BERMLORD, Charlotte, North Carolina

ISBN-13: 978-0991071326 (BERMLORD)
ISBN-10: 0991071328

First Edition, June 2015

Typeset in Garamond
Cover art and design by Lot Aznar
Author photograph courtesy of Mary Ickert of Mary L. Photography

To My Father

I wouldn't be the woman I am today
without first having been your little girl.

"Founded by Thomas Jefferson, the University of Virginia is located in Charlottesville. It's referred to among insiders as Mr. Jefferson's University or simply The University. The school also has its own distinct lingo: The campus is referred to as the "Grounds," the central quad is the "Lawn," and students are either a first, second, third or fourth year. Only first-year students are required to live on campus, and many upperclassmen live in off-campus apartments or fraternity and sorority houses."

U.S News & World Report

Chapter One

Spring Semester – Second Year

I picked up the last card from the stack and placed the three of hearts on the four of spades and the ten of diamonds on the Jack of clubs. One by one, each of the cards found a home on top of its designated suit until four neat piles topped with kings lay on the end table beside me. It had taken me seven tries and the better part of an hour to finish one complete round of solitaire.

"Finally," I said with a burst of relief, readjusting my position as I slid my feet from beneath me back onto the floor so I could turn my attention to Nate.

In the chair on my left, he continued sleeping peacefully. His head was tucked into his chest and a trickle of drool pooled at the corner of his lips. My instinct was to wipe it away, but I knew better than to disturb him. With the stress of the night on top of everything else, there was only one explanation for how he was able to nod off so quickly while the rest of us remained steadfast in our vigil. And although I would have welcomed his company, I could not deny him respite, especially when for him sleep was such a precious commodity.

It had been a difficult year for the two of us. Nothing had been the same since the accident in September, the night Nate changed forever. As I listened to his shallow breathing, it brought me comfort to know that despite his struggles, he was still beside me, even if it was only because I couldn't bring myself to give up on him. He was a whisper of the man I'd fallen in love with our first year, but as I turned to gaze at him, snoring softly through parted lips, there was still a glimmer of the man he used to be. Most nights, even sleep didn't offer relief from the burden of his guilt. I worried for him, although I was out of ideas for ways to help.

His path of self-destruction seemed to have no end.

After suffering for three consecutive hours on the uncomfortable waiting room chair, I stretched my arms above my head and worked at relieving the fatigue in my joints. As I glanced around at my family, it felt selfish to be thinking only of Nate when they were also in need of prayer. The middle of the night phone call from my brother Charlie had been filled with both frantic exuberance and fear. Today would be a big day for him. And for his wife, Brooke. And for me too, I supposed.

Brooke's mother rested awkwardly under the crook of her husband's arm. Their eyes were closed but they weren't asleep. My mom stared blankly at the pages of an outdated magazine, but I hadn't seen her turn a page in over half an hour. She chewed the tip of her thumbnail nervously, humming softly to herself. For everyone's sake, I hoped we wouldn't need to wait much longer to find out what was going on in the ward beyond the double doors.

My stomach growled. The clock on the wall indicated the sun would soon be rising, but there was no natural light in the waiting room, only the harsh glare of the fluorescents overhead. I had just decided to set off for the vending machine around the corner for a donut when Charlie burst through the doors wearing ill-fitting scrubs and a smile that stopped my heart.

Everyone was suddenly wide awake.

"It's a girl!" he cried.

In one swift motion, we crossed the room to him, swept up in the emotion of the moment. Mom wrapped him in her arms, and as tears built in her eyes, the tightness in her jaw released.

"And she's fine? She's going to be okay?" Brooke's mother asked.

"They're both fine," he replied excitedly. "They had to take her via cesarean, as we expected because of the placement of the placenta, so Brooke's gonna have a longer recovery. But the baby, even five weeks premature..." He trailed off, a small smile playing at his lips. "She's itty-bitty but she's perfect."

Brooke's father squeezed Charlie's shoulder affectionately. "When am I going to get to meet this new granddaughter of mine?"

He shook his head and ran his fingers through his tousled hair. "I don't know quite yet. Brooke's been moved to recovery, and they've taken the baby to the NICU just to run some tests and make sure everything's okay. She came out screaming and her APGAR was a nine, so as long as she doesn't need any help breathing, it shouldn't be too long before you can go back."

It didn't surprise me how natural talking about all the baby stuff seemed for Charlie. He'd been a father figure to me long before our father's death, acting as my supportive male role model for as long as I could remember. When he announced Brooke's pregnancy to the family in the fall, everyone else seemed relieved that they had finally decided to start a family. But unlike the others, I was glad they waited a few years into their marriage, giving them more time together as a couple before becoming parents. Both of them had been pushed to grow up too fast too soon, with Brooke's younger brother Branson's untimely death and the unusual circumstances surrounding Charlie's adoption.

But now, after witnessing how attentive he'd been to Brooke throughout the pregnancy, I was certain that it was finally the right time for him to become a father to his own little girl.

I approached my brother, locking eyes with the person I admired most in the world. "So, are you going to tell us now, finally?"

"Tell you what?" he replied playfully, nudging me in the arm.

I smiled at him. "It's time for you to tell us what you've decided to name her. We've waited long enough."

My demand was bolstered by a chorus of agreement from the others, including Nate who had sidled up beside me.

He welled up at the request and bit at his bottom lip to keep the tears at bay.

"It was Brooke's idea, if it was a girl... she wouldn't take no for an answer."

We waited patiently for him to continue.

"We're naming her Victoria," he said finally, "after my mother."

Chapter Two

Fall Semester - First Year

I was dreading the final "Incoming Student Orientation" meeting. Each one I'd attended had been more boring and worthless than the last, but the series of seminars was required so I dragged myself from a blissful rereading of *One Flew Over the Cuckoo's Nest* and headed with my roommate Lesley to the student center.

When I saw him, I was suddenly glad that I'd decided to put down the book.

His eyes were grey, the color of fine pewter. They were the first thing I noticed as I approached because they weren't a real color, like blue or brown or green. They were so unusual I had to consciously force myself to look away so he didn't think I was crazy for staring at them. But I hadn't averted my gaze fast enough.

"My mom's eyes are the same color," he said smiling, in a way that wasn't necessarily conceited, but just to tell me, so I knew.

I allowed myself to look again as I sat down beside him, not because I wanted to, but because I needed to make sure I hadn't imagined them.

Pewter. They were real.

I smiled at him. Tried to recover some shred of dignity. "I guess she can't deny you then," I laughed feebly, feeling overwhelmed by the luck of our pairing.

He cocked his head to the side and smirked at me. "Isn't that what they say about dads? If you look like your dad, he can't deny you? But my mom actually gave birth to me, so it would be pretty hard to deny that, wouldn't it?" He chuckled to himself.

Based on his appearance alone I assumed he was laughing at my expense. When I noticed the biceps squeezed into the arms of his football jersey, I was certain of it. My heart sank at the thought of being partnered with some gorgeous jock, probably fresh off the starting lineup, who now thought I was an idiot. I tried to change the subject.

"Do you have practice after this?" I asked, unfolding the questionnaire we were supposed to complete together.

"Yeah. I might actually have to leave early to get there on time. I was hoping I didn't have to come here at all, but Coach didn't give us a choice." He fished a pencil out of his backpack. "I'm Nate, by the way. Nate Johansen."

"Melody Johnson," I replied, searching my bag for my own pen. "That explains why we're together - alphabetical order." I rolled my eyes. "Really original, orientation leaders."

He didn't respond but I could feel him looking at me. I felt my ears redden despite my best efforts to remain calm. "Melody," he repeated, ignoring the rest of what I'd said. "Like a song?"

I didn't know how to react. Was he making fun of me again?

"Yeah, I guess," I said finally, unnerved by his proximity and my sudden lack of intellect.

"I like it," he said, as if his approval should count for something.

I admitted silently to myself that it did.

We worked together for the better part of an hour, filling out the survey about our orientation experience. I had a hard time keeping myself from staring at him. In addition to his piercing eyes, he was huge, like a boulder. I felt like a wisp of air beside him. I wanted desperately for him not to be a dumb jock so I could feel justified in liking him. Sadly, he wasn't making it easy, with his snarky responses to each of the questions and repeated threats to write in his own inappropriate answers involving bathroom humor and sexual innuendos. I was initially annoyed by his childlike behavior, but eventually realized he was merely trying to make me laugh. When I let down my guard and gave in to his irreverent humor, I was rewarded with his wisdom.

"How would you rate the food services department?" he read aloud. "Where's the 'blows chunks' option? Seriously. Let me write that in. Their meatloaf on Tuesday had to be made of horse."

I couldn't help it. I cracked a smile. "It was pretty gross, wasn't it?"

He grimaced, pretending to be sick. "It was disgusting. No amount of ketchup could've saved it."

I shook my head and slid the paper in his direction. "Go ahead! Write in 'blows chunks.' What do I care?"

I watched as he wrote the words BLOWS CHUNKS carefully in block letters. He was overly pleased with himself.

"You're funny," I said, not realizing until the words escaped that I'd spoken them aloud.

Nate cocked his head at me. "My mom says I need to be more serious. You know, take life seriously cuz I'm in college now and football scholarship and big career and blah, blah, blah." He gestured with his hands, making air quotes, which for some reason I found ridiculously charming. "But I don't know. Life should be fun, shouldn't it? If it's not fun, why bother?"

I considered his perspective, reflecting on my own situation. "She has a point though. We're not kids anymore. And I get that we have to figure stuff out and grow up…"

He held up his hands before tossing his pencil into his backpack. "Stop right there. You're bringing me down, Mel."

I panicked, afraid that he would leave thinking we had nothing in common. "You didn't let me finish. I was going to say I feel like there should be a way to do both. I was agreeing with you." I sighed. "For the past couple years, I've been so focused on keeping up my grades and getting into school, I haven't had much time for fun. I could honestly use some more fun in my life."

"Really?"

"Yeah. Really." I paused. "Are you making fun of me again?"

He furrowed his brow with a look of genuine curiosity. "What do you mean *again*? I haven't made fun of you at all."

I was skeptical. He seemed exactly like the type of person who would delight in making fun of other people. "Seriously? The comment about your mom denying you and my name is a song? You've been laughing at me all afternoon."

He became serious for the first time since I'd taken the seat beside him. "I wasn't making fun of you, Melody."

I looked away but could feel him scrutinizing me, as if his eyes were piercing right through me. Finally, I worked up the courage to face him, but regarded him suspiciously, the way a mouse observes a cat. "You weren't?"

"No. Why would I?"

I hesitated. "I don't know," I said finally as I zipped up my bag. I really didn't have an answer beyond the fact that I sort of always assumed other people found advantages where they could and many times that meant bringing other people down. My father had built a career on it.

There was an awkward silence as he stood up from his chair.

"I might be just what you're looking for, if you're looking for some fun. And I'm not kidding." He looked at his phone. "I'm late for practice. Which dorm are you in?"

I couldn't imagine why he was asking. "Kellogg. Over in Alderman."

"What room?"

I had to think for a second. "Two-eleven."

"Okay." He started to amble away but then looked back over his shoulder to wave goodbye. "Maybe I'll stop by."

Chapter Three

Spring Semester – Second Year

Nate and I slipped away to the hospital cafeteria in search of breakfast after the nurse announced it would be another hour before Brooke and Victoria would be ready to receive visitors. His hand was clammy against mine, indicating he was beginning to experience symptoms of withdrawal. By this point, I knew the drill. Within minutes, he would slink away, deluding himself into believing I didn't realize where he was going or what he was doing. But I knew. I'd known for months.

It started small, as most things do. The reaction to a trauma. To not knowing what to do or what to say or how to feel. In hushed voices and behind closed doors. It started as a way to cope. Nothing more. Nothing less.

Now it was all there was.

We reached the entrance to the cafeteria and I perused our options. There were the usual suspects - cold cereal, powdered eggs, and greasy hash browns. I spotted a bowl of fresh fruit at the far end of the line.

"You want a banana?" I asked, looking up at him without taking my hand from his. "Maybe a carton of orange juice?"

As we stood together in the suffocating cafeteria, his beautiful eyes were barely visible behind drooping lids. He was with me and not with me at the same time.

"Nate," I repeated when he didn't respond, "you want something to eat?"

He let go of my hand and fished around in his pockets. He wasn't feeling for his wallet or his phone. He was digging for pills.

"Yeah," he responded finally. Get me whatever you're getting. I'm gonna find the bathroom. I'll be right back."

I shuffled to the front of the cafeteria line, my stomach in knots about what Nate was off pretending not to do. I selected two blueberry muffins, a carton of orange juice, an apple, and two bananas from the bowl, but upon reaching the register, realized I didn't have enough cash to pay for it all. The twenty dollar bills I'd gotten from the ATM the night before had disappeared, and I had no doubt about who had taken them or why. It wasn't the first-time money had gone missing over the past six months. Initially, I thought I was being forgetful, but Nate had grown sloppy as his addiction intensified and he'd become lazy about covering his tracks. And so, as my stomach grumbled, I bought what I could afford with the handful of singles that remained and found an empty table beside a window to wait for him to return.

I warmed my face in the sunlight streaming through the glass and watched the family beside me. They exuded an air of relief, despite bearing tear-stained cheeks, and I wondered what ordeal they'd survived as I watched Nate thread his way through the throngs of doctors and nurses grabbing a bite before beginning their shifts. He spotted me on the far side of the room and the bench shifted as he slid into the booth beside me.

"Feeling better?" I asked more sternly than I intended as I turned to face him.

He picked at a thread hanging from the cargo pocket of his shorts. "Not today, Mel. You know I didn't sleep. You're the one who came and woke me in the middle of the night, remember?"

I remembered. I remembered barely being able to rouse him. After calling repeatedly and pounding on his bedroom door until I'd woken all of his roommates, I finally resorted to picking the lock.

A STRAW MAN

What I found nearly brought me to tears. I'd never seen him looking so much like a corpse.

He carefully peeled the banana I slid across the table as a peace offering. "Thanks," he mumbled through his first mouthful.

I picked at my muffin and considered what to say. I'd confronted him before about the pills and the stealing and each time he shut me out. He didn't want help. He was punishing himself. I decided not to drag his demons into the light of the hospital cafeteria.

"I'm an aunt," I said finally, forcing myself to be cheerful.

"She's a lucky little girl," he replied.

"I wonder what she looks like?"

"I guess we'll see in a little while." He paused, peeling his banana a bit further. "Don't be surprised if she looks like a monkey though."

His comment caught me off guard. It had been a long time since he'd cracked a joke. I couldn't resist playing along, thankful for these glimmers of the past, as fleeting as they had become.

"What?" I gasped, feigning anger. "I'll have you know there hasn't been a single monkey in our family in at least four generations."

"Maybe she'll be a throwback." He took another bite. "Monkey is recessive."

I shook my head. It was nice to see him smile and even nicer to hear him laugh. It felt almost like our first year. Second year had been another story altogether. Thinking about it reminded me of final exams.

"We were supposed to be studying today," I said, changing the subject. "So much for that."

He shrugged his shoulders. "It wasn't going to help me anyway. Even if I ace them all, the best I can hope for is a D average."

"You can retake biology this summer. If you do well, they might still let you play in the fall."

He shoved the last bite of banana in his mouth, chewed and swallowed before responding. "I'm not gonna play next year."

"But you might still be able to…"

"I'm not playing either way." He looked out the window, unwilling to meet my gaze. "I already told you that."

I took a sip of orange juice and resisted the urge to break into full-blown mother mode. "I know that's what you said. I just thought maybe it would be good for you to be out there, with the rest of the team, having fun like you used to."

"Sam doesn't get to be out there, having fun like he used to, does he?" Nate snapped.

I bowed my head. I'd hit a nerve. "It wasn't your fault," I whispered for the hundredth time.

"It was all my fault," he replied.

Victoria, as it turned out, didn't look anything like a monkey. She was terribly small, weighing just over five pounds, but she was perfect and precious in every way. As she lay sleeping in my arms, I could think of no better reason to blow off studying for my American Politics final.

The family had gathered in Brooke's hospital room just after she was released from recovery. There were more people than seats, so a bench had been dragged from the hallway for her parents while my mother sat in the only chair in the corner of the room. Nate perched precariously on the window ledge between the floral arrangements and gift baskets stuffed with balloons and teddy bears, the proverbial bull in a sea of breakable things. I stood beside him, unconsciously swaying the baby as I rocked from side to side.

"You're a natural, Melody," Charlie said from across the room where he was curled up on the tiny hospital bed with Brooke.

"Only while she's sleeping," I replied. "As soon as she cries, I'm giving her back."

As I adjusted the tiny knitted cap Victoria wore, I considered everything in life that had come together to ensure her creation.

The story of Brooke and Charlie's romance was a legend retold countless times at every possible family event. Christmas, birthdays, their wedding, Fourth of July... inevitably someone would bring up the tale of their happily-ever-after. Everyone knew how Brooke took multiple trips back in time to save her brother's life, accidentally meeting Charlie along the way. But of course, when things didn't work out as she intended, she was forced to let them both go in order to preserve her own timeline. In the end, we were all glad Fate had different plans, ensuring the two were reunited later on, without the help of time travel.

Years later, Charlie nearly ruined everything by taking his own trip back in time when he attempted to find his birth mother, Victoria. I still felt partially responsible for encouraging him to track her down through space and time. Unfortunately, he'd inadvertently saved her life in the process and was sentenced to fifteen years in prison for breaking one of the most highly punishable traveling rules. Luckily for Brooke and Charlie, Fate stepped in once again in the form of Victoria, who took her own trip back in time to restore the original timeline.

As a result of all the turmoil, he ended up proposing to Brooke before she'd even graduated from college. We all thought he was nuts, committing to marriage at such a young age, but he wouldn't be dissuaded. Love makes you do crazy things.

I should know.

It was clear to all of us that Vicki's birth was nothing short of a full-blown miracle, knowing the number of timelines where Fate intervened to ensure her existence. She wriggled in her blanket and scrunched her tiny face into something between a grimace and a smile. And then she opened her eyes.

"Hey, Vicki," I cooed as she stared vacantly past my head.

"She can't really see you," Brooke said. "Her eyes aren't fully developed yet. She might recognize your voice though."

I whispered to her about how pretty she was and what fun we would have when she was able. And then, like a demon possessed, she began to wail.

"She sounds hungry," Mom said.

"And it certainly doesn't sound like she's having any trouble with her lungs," Brooke's father added as I delivered the squirmy bundle into Brooke's arms.

Nate coughed loudly from the window ledge which I took as an indication that he was ready to leave. It broke my heart to know that obligation, not desire, was what kept him by my side. He was only at the hospital because after almost two years together, some small piece inside still considered himself part of my family. I missed the days when he enjoyed spending time with all of them, especially Charlie, but even their relationship had become increasingly estranged as his addiction grew. Gone were the days of week-long visits, holiday celebrations, and family vacations. Now he was more comfortable being alone with his pain than among the warmth of a loving family.

I was torn about leaving. Being with Brooke and Charlie felt safe. They were easy. They weren't constantly reminding me that my love would never be enough to compensate for the pain of loss. And on top of everything else, I wasn't ready to say goodbye to Vicki. But it had been a long day, and I knew beyond the three-hour drive back to school, I still had a full night of studying ahead of me.

And of course, Nate was ready to go.

"Since you have to feed her, I guess it's a good time for us to head back," I relented.

I gave the baby a kiss on the head and ran my fingers against her petal-soft cheek. As I turned from the bed, Charlie reached for my hand.

"I'm glad you came, Mel," he said, sensing my sadness. "Just do well on your finals and then you can come hang out whenever you want this summer."

I smiled at him. He knew how difficult spring semester had been for me, both academically and emotionally. He knew I needed a break even if I was reluctant to take one.

But Nate needed me too. I couldn't just walk away.

"Thanks," I said. "Next weekend. I promise."

Brooke gave me a knowing wink and her parents waved as I joined Nate in the doorway.

"Congratulations," he said to my family. "She's beautiful."

"Thanks," Charlie said. "And you're welcome to come visit too, Nate. Anytime."

I felt for his hand and curled my fingers beneath his. He rocked nervously in his sneakers. It was time to go.

He lagged behind as we made our way silently through the parking garage. At six foot-five and two hundred-thirty pounds, Nate was an average size football player. Off the field however, he seemed enormous. The difference in our size was something people seemed obliged to comment on, as if we wouldn't notice without it being pointed out, so it felt strange when the parking attendant didn't say a word as we walked past. It made me sad to think that perhaps he didn't realize we were together and made me long for the days when people could tell just by looking that we were a couple. Sometimes it didn't seem so long ago. Sometimes it seemed like a lifetime.

Chapter Four
Fall Semester-First Year

Although first year students were forbidden from having cars at school, Nate managed to sweet-talk a woman who owned an adjacent property into giving him a parking spot at her house. Two days after our first meeting, he attempted to impress me by suggesting going into town for dinner, away from the dining hall's questionable entrees. The hostess at the restaurant was the first person to ever comment on our height difference.

"How's that work?" she asked before taking our names for the waiting list.

"How's what work?" I replied.

Her eyes darted between us. "You two. He's what, two feet taller than you?" She winked. "I bet that's interesting."

I hadn't known how to respond and stood paralyzed, my mouth gaping open. Luckily, Nate came to the rescue.

"Usually I just push her around in our baby stroller, but tonight she threw such a fit when I tried to put her in, I just gave up and let her walk. What're ya gonna do?" He shrugged his shoulders.

I grinned up at him. He *was* funny. And kind of irreverent. But he stood up for me so how could I not like him?

After instructing me to choose whatever toppings I wanted for the pizza, I watched as he systematically pulled off every mushroom from the slices on his plate.

"We could've gotten it half and half," I said.

"Nah. I don't mind. You want them? Extra toppings for you that way."

He slid the mushrooms onto my plate and devoured his first slice. He was an eating machine. Even at the height of swim or soccer seasons, I'd never seen Charlie eat so quickly.

"Don't tell me you're one of those girls who doesn't eat," he remarked as I gaped at him with my pizza raised in midair.

I took a bite, chewed, and swallowed deliberately before giving him the satisfaction of an answer. "I eat, thank you very much. I just choose not to inhale my food."

He set his pizza back on the plate and considered me from across the table, boring a hole into me with his pewter eyes. "I'm the youngest of eight," he said matter-of-factly.

I was taken aback. "Eight?"

"Yeah, eight. And when you have seven older brothers and sisters who are faster than you and bigger than you, you learn real quick to get all the food you can and eat it fast before somebody snatches it away from you." Dimples formed at the corners of his mouth as he waited for my reaction. His smile was amazing.

"I can't imagine what that would be like," I said, shaking my head in disbelief.

He sat back in the booth and cocked his head to the side. "It would be like musical chairs but with food. There's never quite enough to go around, so you better get what you can before the music stops and you're the one left without a chair. Or a sandwich."

I took a sip of my soda. "It looks to me as though you managed to get plenty. You certainly don't seem malnourished, that's for sure."

He laughed. A deep, throaty laugh that reminded me of the way my grandfather sounded when he played with me as a child.

"What exactly are you saying, Mel?" he asked, his eyes twinkling. "Are you telling me I'm fat?"

"No." I took another bite of pizza. "Just that somewhere along the line, you must have started being the bigger, faster one."

"Maybe," he said. "I really think they all just grew up and moved out, one by one. But my mom still only knew how to cook for a small army, so by the time I was a teenager and there were only two of us left, there was plenty for me and Will."

"So how big's Will?"

"He's about my size. We're the tallest of the boys. Joe, Adam, and Ben are all around six-foot-one or six-foot-two."

"Shrimps," I said.

"Don't tell them that. My sisters are smaller, of course. Beth, Kay, and Alice. They're all like five-foot-nine. Maybe a little taller."

"You're a family of giants!" I declared.

He laughed again and helped himself to another slice of pizza. "What about your family?" he asked.

I thought for a moment. What about my family? There was so much to tell. Was it prudent to tell the truth to this guy I barely knew?

I decided to go for broke.

"My family's about average in size, but they tend to be a little complicated," I began.

"Whose isn't?"

I wiped the corners of my mouth with a paper napkin. "No. Mine's actually extremely complicated, and I don't really know where to start. You're probably the first person I've ever had to explain them to, since everyone in my home town already knows about them. We were kind of all over the news at one point."

"Am I dating some sort of a celebrity?"

Were we dating? My heart fluttered involuntarily inside my chest.

"Is this a date?" I asked.

"Yes," he replied without a moment's hesitation.

"Uh, then no. You are not dating some sort of celebrity. You may have heard of my father though."

"Who's your father? Please tell me he's not a homicidal maniac or something."

Close but not quite, I thought. That would be my grandfather.

"His name was Phil Johnson. He was the Virginia senator who died during a climbing expedition about five years ago."

Nate's expression softened. "I don't remember anything about it. I'm not big into politics, but I'm really sorry to hear about your dad."

I picked at the extra mushrooms Nate kept tossing on my plate. "It's okay. It was a really weird time for all of us. I still have my mom and my older brother, Charlie. The funny thing is that Charlie is only my half-brother, but we didn't know it while we were growing up. We thought we were full brother and sister, but when my dad died, we discovered from my mom that Charlie was actually adopted. He went searching for his birth parents and discovered that our dad was actually his biological father. So even though for a little while we thought we weren't blood related, it turned out he's my half-brother after all." I took another sip of soda and wondered how ridiculous I sounded to Nate, who sat staring at me as though I'd grown another head.

He took a deep breath and leaned in across the table toward me. "So what you're telling me is your dad had a baby with someone else and then he and your mom adopted the baby?"

"Yes."

"And that's your brother, Charlie?"

"Yup."

He threw his arms in the air. "Your mom's a saint!" he declared.

I couldn't have agreed more. "She didn't know at the time that she was raising her husband's illegitimate child, but yes, she is."

"Well," he said, finishing off the last bite of crust and pushing back from the table, "your family's really something."

"Someday maybe I'll tell you about my sister-in-law. I don't want to scare you away though."

"I don't scare easily. I just can't believe there's more."

"Another story for another time."

The waitress arrived with the bill. Nate snatched it from my hand.

"I told you this was a date, remember? I'm paying." He wouldn't take no for an answer and I didn't protest for too long.

As we said our goodbyes on the front steps of my dorm, it occurred to me that we really didn't have anything in common with one another. He was easy to talk to and easier to look at, but he was popular. Played football. Was adored by the masses.

And I wasn't.

So while I expected him to cross me off his registry of available co-eds and move on to the next girl on the list, I was surprised to discover that having nothing in common with me didn't seem to matter to him. And it turned out that it must not have mattered to me either since I quickly agreed to join him and his teammates for a movie marathon later in the week.

"I don't know that I'm actually going to fit in with your friends," I worried aloud as he sat beside me on the stoop. I'd chosen libraries over athletic fields at every opportunity growing up. Now I was going to be expected to fraternize with people who knew which games were played in quarters and which were played in periods. My head spun just thinking about it.

"They're all pretty much just like me. Tons of fun," he said. "And as I recall, you said you were looking for some fun." He hoisted himself from the step and reached for my hand to pull me up beside him. "So, are you in or not?"

"I guess I'm in," I replied, wondering what exactly I was signing myself up for and how I was going to make it until Wednesday without seeing him again.

He took two steps down the stairs toward the sidewalk, and just as I thought he was going to leave without saying goodbye, he turned to face me. We were almost nose to nose and without any further warning, he reached around to place his hand on the small of my back and kissed me. It was sweet and soft and completely different from the way I'd been kissed by other boys in the past. This boy knew what he was doing and I realized immediately that I was in really, really, big trouble.

"I'm glad you're in," he said, grinning from ear to ear when he finally released me from his embrace. "Maybe I'll see you around tomorrow. Hopefully."

"Ok," I replied, unable to manage any higher level of communication.

He leapt down the last three steps and began ambling across the Grounds in the direction of his dorm. I stood like an idiot, watching him walk away until he was no longer illuminated by the streetlamps and the darkness of night completely engulfed him. Only then did I realize I was holding my breath.

Chapter Five

Spring Semester — Second Year

"We're here," I whispered to Nate as I shut off the car's engine in front of his apartment. He'd fallen asleep in the passenger's seat five minutes after leaving the hospital and continued snoring softly into his chest the entire trip. I nudged him gently on the shoulder. "Nate?"

He roused slowly. He was groggy. Groggier than I'd seen him in a while. I wondered how many Vicodin he'd taken before we got in the car.

He stirred. "Mel?"

"Yeah. We're here. You want me to walk you in?"

He opened his eyes and leaned toward me across the console, not yet fully lucid. "I love you. I don't deserve you. I'm sorry for everything."

I kissed him gently on the lips and waited for him to come to. "I love you too. But don't just be sorry. Try to fix it. You can get better. Summer's here." I hesitated. "Go to the treatment center."

He pulled away, slowly waking up. "I'm fine. There's nothing that needs fixing. Nothing I can't handle. I'm just..." He trailed off.

"I know. You're having trouble sleeping."

"Yes. I'm still working through it. I'm sure I'll be feeling better soon."

I took a deep breath as I lifted his chin, forcing him to look at me. The color of his eyes betrayed him. The radiance of pewter had been replaced by the ashen grey of soot, and my heart broke to think of his sorrow. "It's been almost a year. You've been saying that since September."

He groaned. "Please. Not now, Mel. Let's just get through finals and then maybe we can talk about it again. Until then, I don't want to think about September. Or Sam. Or football. Or any of it. I just want it to go away."

That was always his response. Just make it go away. But I couldn't make it go away. No one could.

Finals were finals. I got through them. I studied. I concentrated as well as could be expected. I prayed for the best.

I don't think Nate even managed the praying part. When I showed up at his apartment at the end of the week, I found him stuffing dirty clothes into a giant duffle bag.

"How'd you do?" I asked from the doorway of his bedroom, content to stay on the periphery of his packing.

He disappeared beneath his bed and reappeared with a wadded-up pair of shorts. "I don't want to talk about it. I just need to get outta here," he said, shoving them into his bag.

I considered offering to help when two of his roommates tore through the front door into the apartment.

"Hey, Melody," Tyree called when he noticed me standing in the hall. "Have a great summer!"

"Thanks," I replied, mustering as much enthusiasm as I could. "You too."

"Are you all finished?" Josh asked as he slid past me into the room.

"Yeah. You?"

"Yeah. Thank God. Time to pack up and head home. At least we're gonna be in this same apartment again next year so I don't have to pack so much. The TV can stay, the sofa, the bed..." He paused, considering Nate's haggard form hunched over his belongings. "Speaking of that, are you in again? I need your deposit if you are."

Nate didn't stop what he was doing. He also didn't respond.

"Yo, Nate, are you in or out?"

I watched as he closed his eyes. I knew he was willing us to go away.

"I'm out, dude," he said finally.

I took hold of the doorknob to steady myself. I couldn't believe he hadn't told me what he was planning. Even with everything he'd been through, I hadn't expected him to just give up. From the look on his face, neither had Josh. We both just stood there, dumbfounded by the reality of what was happening. No one wanted to acknowledge it had come to this. Neither of us was willing to accept that Nate was dropping out of school, even though he had already dropped out of life.

"But why?" Josh said at last.

Nate struggled with the zipper, swearing under his breath. "It's complicated."

Josh and I exchanged a knowing glance. We were both aware of why he wasn't coming back and knew Nate lacked the courage to say the words aloud.

"Sam wouldn't want it to be like this," Josh said quietly.

"You're right," Nate replied. "He wouldn't want to be dead."

Chapter Six

Fall Semester – Second Year

It was steamy; unusually hot for the first week of September. My windows were open and the fan on my desk blew directly into my face. There was no central air in my dorm and although it hadn't been a problem in the past, I suddenly wished I had followed Nate's lead to live off Grounds in an air-conditioned apartment. As I sat thinking of him, he appeared in my doorway, dressed in his orange team jersey and blue athletic shorts. His chest and shoulders were enormous, even without the pads underneath. The rush of adrenaline that always accompanied his arrival coursed through my body. I never got tired of seeing him, tan and perfectly rough around the edges, as he threw himself across my bed, sending my Spanish homework fluttering to the floor.

"Hey, you," he said.

"Hey, yourself," I replied, restacking my assignment. "Don't you have practice?"

"Not 'til 4:30. No pads practice today since we have the game tomorrow. Coach said he only needs about an hour to run over the plays one more time and to go over any changes in the lineup." He positioned himself so he was sitting upright against my headboard. "With all my free time I thought I'd stop by and bother you for a while, and it looks like I arrived just in time." He pointed to my large stack of books. "Are you doing homework on a Friday afternoon?"

"No. Yes. Maybe a little bit," I said as I climbed onto his lap. "I'm just trying to make sure I stay on top of things." He fingered the top button of my shirt. "If you're looking for something to stay on top of, you can stay on top of me all afternoon. I gotta be honest though, finding you here like this has me a little bit concerned. Have you learned nothing from me? Do you need remedial training?" He coughed dramatically, brandishing his hands in the air. "Repeat after me. Friday nights are not for homework."

"Friday nights are not for homework," I parroted to appease him.

"Friday nights are for fun."

"Friday nights are for fun."

He nodded approvingly. "Good. Now that we have that settled, what plans do you have for this evening?"

I didn't know. I hadn't really thought about it. "I guess I have to eat dinner. I'll wait for you if you want or I'll go earlier if you're planning to eat with the team."

He pulled me close and kissed me playfully on the nose. "I spend way too much time with those goons. I'd rather eat dinner with you. Wanna hit the grill?"

One of the things I loved most about Nate was that he wasn't embarrassed to make his feelings about me known. He didn't hide our relationship from his friends, and he didn't make excuses for wanting to spend time with me. He just did what he wanted to do, regardless of what anyone else thought of him. And it made me swoon that what he wanted to do was spend time with me.

"Can Lesley come too?"

He chuckled. "Doesn't she always? You two are attached at the hip. It's like getting two girlfriends in one."

"Bonus for you," I said as I settled down beside him and turned on the TV. "Why don't you see if Sam wants to come too."

"Please don't tell me you're going to waste more time trying to get them together again this year," he groaned. "Lesley's so moody and judgmental. There's no way he'll ever go out with her.

Sometimes I honestly don't know how you two are such good friends."

"She's not that bad," I said, coming to Lesley's defense. "Maybe hooking up with Sam would help make her less… volatile."

Nate shook his head. "That's an interesting choice of words. I might have used crazy instead. And besides, your plan to get them together didn't work last year. Why should this year be any different?"

"Because Sam was still pining over that horrible Jada girl last year and now he's not. He told me she met someone over the summer and it's serious, so it's time for him to get over her. Sam and Lesley could be perfect for each other. I just have to get them to realize it."

He smiled at me, shaking his head. "You're too good for that girl, you know that? And besides, relationships need to develop organically. You can't force them. They have to happen like you and me."

I rolled over and propped myself onto my elbow so I could look directly at him. "First, since when do you use the word 'organically' to describe an evolving relationship? And second, how do you know our meeting wasn't a set up?"

He turned away from the TV and pulled me into his arms before rolling on top of me in one fluid motion, pinning me beneath him as he supported his own weight. If I hadn't known he didn't want to hurt me, I would have been petrified.

"You think the Freshman Orientation Gods planned for you to fall in love with me?" he asked, his breath warm on my face.

"No," I replied, pushing on his chest with all of my strength. "I think they planned for *you* to fall in love with *me*. Now get off me so I can finish my Spanish."

Instead of yielding to my pleas, he released his arms, crushing me beneath him.

"Get off!" I squealed.

He laughed, holding himself just high enough on his elbows to keep from smothering me completely. "Never!" he cried.

I began tickling under his ribs, hoping it would entice him to release me, but it only served to make him more determined.

"This isn't a fair fight," I managed to squeak as he covered my face with kisses.

At that moment Lesley stumbled through the doorway, her arms heavy with books from the library. She sighed as she dropped them to the floor.

"Are you two at it again?" she asked, wriggling free of her backpack.

"Not again," he quipped, relenting control and sitting up. "Still."

"You two are cute but some days you make me want to puke," Lesley said matter-of-factly. "How about keeping the saccharine to a minimum, huh?"

"How can I resist this adorable little face?" Nate teased, pinching my cheeks between both of his hands.

"Seriously. Enough. I'm nauseous over here."

I gave Nate a stern look, putting an end to his banter. "So," I said, changing the subject as I climbed off the bed, "Nate and I are going to the grill after his practice and he's bringing Sam. You'll come too, right?"

"Will I have more of this to look forward to?"

I glared at Nate as he opened his mouth to respond. "We will be on our best behavior, won't we Nathan?"

He pretended to shine his halo. "On my honor."

"Fine. I'll go. But only because Sam will be there to run interference."

We arranged to meet up at six at the front entrance to the grill, but by 6:30 Lesley and I decided the boys weren't coming. We ate cheesesteaks by ourselves and were almost back to our room when a text arrived from Nate. My shoulders sagged as I illuminated the screen.

Practice sucked. Came home to shower and crash. Sorry about dinner. Raincheck? Call u in the AM.

I clicked off my phone, shoved it in my pocket, and continued walking along the sidewalk.

"Everything okay?" Lesley asked as she fell into step beside me.

"I guess."

"That doesn't sound reassuring. Was that Nate?"

"Yeah."

"And?"

I sighed, unable to mask my disappointment. "I guess something happened at practice that's got him upset, and he just doesn't feel like hanging out."

We walked in silence as the excitement and anticipation of Friday night buzzed around us. Groups of students moved like small herds of cattle carting cases of beer to various parties on and off Grounds.

"We could just go do something ourselves," she said finally in an attempt to lift my spirits. "Sasha and Alex are heading over to the Phi Delt house. We could go with them. Or I heard in biology class today that Sigma Pi is doing something too and I'm already on their list. Or if you don't want to go out we could rent a movie and stay in with whoever's on the floor."

Although I appreciated her attempts to distract me, my mind was racing in a million directions as I tried to convince myself there was no reason to feel dejected.

Nate and I spent the summer between our first and second years living with our respective families almost two hours away from one another. During that time, we saw as much of each other as we possibly could, scheduling visits around summer jobs and family obligations. He spent fourth of July weekend celebrating with my family in Washington DC and even came with us on our annual beach trip. Even still, I discovered not having him physically present in my everyday life was tough. I blamed my father for the jealousy and trust issues I projected onto my relationship with Nate, but more than anything else, my lack of self-confidence fueled my fears. I worried endlessly over the summer that he would forget about me or find someone else, and although those fears were unfounded, they continued to linger, just beneath the surface.

And so my initial reaction to Nate's text was to wonder if his excuse was as innocent as it appeared. Life taught me that many people simply lied to solve their problems, and I needed to be mindful if I was to avoid being deceived. Although Nate had never given me a reason to doubt him, a nagging voice in the back of my head always caused me to wonder. Was he really crashing at home or was he choosing something or someone else over me?

We reached the steps of our building and Lesley waited patiently for me to respond.

"Mel, he's a good guy. He loves you. I'm sure whatever is going on will be fine by morning."

I didn't respond. I knew she was right. I silently chastised myself for focusing immediately on my own feelings instead of considering how bad things must have gone at practice for Nate to opt out of a Friday night of fun. I pulled my phone out of my pocket.

Sorry practice didn't go well. Rest up for the game tomorrow and I'll see you in the morning. I love you.

I hit send and grabbed Lesley's hand.

"Sigma Pi, huh?"

"Yeah. You wanna go?"

My phone chirped. I glanced at the screen.

I love you too. Til tomorrow...

I looked at Lesley. "Absolutely," I replied.

Chapter Seven

Summer Break – Second to Third Year

For the fifth day in a row I found myself at Brooke and Charlie's house with baby Vicki curled up in my arms. There was no end to the love I felt for my niece, so petite and perfect swaddled in her gingham blanket. I watched Brooke move gingerly around the kitchen making sandwiches, still recovering from her cesarean. We were all very relieved that both she and the baby were doing well after Vicki's unexpected early arrival into the world.

"Egg salad again today, or something else?" Brooke asked as she pulled out the loaf of bread from the pantry.

"Egg salad sounds good, but I should really be the one making lunch for you," I replied.

She opened the refrigerator and grabbed a jar of mayo from the shelf. "Stop. I've got this. It's just so nice to be up and about again. And besides, Vicki is quite comfortable right where she is. Best not to disturb her as long as she's sleeping."

She slid my sandwich across the counter and I carefully positioned myself with the baby in one arm so I could eat with my other hand. Working one-handed took some getting used to and I ended up losing half my sandwich into my lap.

"You're a mess," Brooke giggled.

"A small price to pay," I replied.

"You'll need to change now before work this afternoon. You can borrow something of mine if you want."

"Thanks," I replied, popping the last bite of my sandwich into my mouth. "Speaking of work, when are you going back to the clinic?"

She shook her head. "I'm trying not to think about it. I know Dr. Barnes and Dr. Fletcher are swamped without me there, but I can't stand the thought of not being home with her right now. The new vet we hired isn't going to be here until September, which would have been fine if Vicki had made it to her due date, but since she came early, I guess I'm going to have to go back full time until he gets here. I can scale back to a couple days a week once he arrives, but until then I really need to get back. I just don't know what I'm going to do with Vicki. We hadn't prepared for this scenario."

I smiled at the precious bundle in my arms. "I'll keep her."

She hesitated. "No. Melody, I can't ask you to do that."

"You're not asking. I'm offering."

She considered me from across the kitchen. "What about working at the campaign office?"

I shrugged my shoulders. I didn't care nearly as much about the campaign as I did about Vicki. "My hours are pretty flexible. I can work evenings. It would be fine."

I saw her resolve wavering. "What about Nate?"

Her question caught me off-guard, but I knew she was referring to whether or not he would be spending time around the baby. I'd confided in both her and Charlie about Nate's worsening condition, and she made it clear that she didn't think we should continue our relationship.

As I gazed down at Vicki, I realized that perhaps she wasn't the only one who felt that way. We'd spoken only once since leaving school the week before, and the conversation consisted of stilted small-talk sandwiched between awkward silence, culminating in a full-blown fight during which he accused me of nagging and I accused him of being a pathetic junkie. I'd begged him to find a job, take a class, or at least attend an NA meeting, but my pestering fell on deaf ears.

"What about him?" I replied at last.

She took a deep breath. I could see she was planning her words carefully which made me nervous.

"Is he coming to visit this summer like he did last year?"

We'd barely discussed it, making only vague promises to one another regarding our loose-knit plans. There were no dates circled and highlighted with smiley faces on my calendar, and my heart ached to think of it, knowing his addiction continued to widen the rift between us. I knew in my heart there would be no visits unless I went to him, and I couldn't imagine what that would look like. Certainly nothing like our trip to the beach the year before.

"I don't know. Maybe. Why?"

She chewed her bottom lip and looked past me, into the family room.

"It's just that I don't know if I want him around the baby. The way he is. It might not be safe."

Although I understood her protective nature, her accusation still felt like a kick to the gut. A small ember of rage sparked inside me ready to defend him. I'd been making excuses for his behavior for months, to his professors, his teammates, and his friends. I'd come up with dozens of ways to explain away his lies as well as his aloof demeanor and rudeness. I'd begged for understanding and compassion, given all he'd been through. It was exhausting.

I was exhausted.

I closed my eyes and willed the tears behind my lids to remain there. I didn't want to burden Brooke with my problems. They weren't her responsibility.

Vicki suddenly began squirming, arching her back as she let out a wail. I looked down to see her beautiful face distort into a scowl. She was awake and she was angry. It suddenly occurred to me that I was angry too.

"I'm sorry, Melody," Brooke said as she positioned herself on the stool beside me at the counter with a bottle and took Vicki from my arms. "I shouldn't have said anything. I didn't mean to upset you."

We sat together in silence while Vicki drank noisily from her bottle. The steady rhythm of her sucking calmed my nerves.

"You don't need to apologize," I said finally, "because you're right about Nate." I searched for just the right word to describe why I didn't want him near the baby either. "He's become untrustworthy."

Brooke held Vicki to her chest and patted gently on her back. "Do you want to talk about it?"

No. I didn't want to talk about it. But I decided maybe I needed to.

"I don't know what there is to say," I began. "He lies to me about where he is and what he's doing. He steals from me constantly, thinking I won't notice. For weeks, I thought I lost the ring Grandma gave me for my sixteenth birthday, but now I'm pretty sure Nate sold it for pills. The worst part is he had the nerve to ask me if you were a full-fledged doctor who could write prescriptions. I swear he would steal your prescription pad if he could get his hands on it." I hesitated, crushed by the guilt of painting him in such a horrible light. I could have told her about dozens of cruel things he'd said and done to me since becoming an addict, but I couldn't bring myself to continue speaking so poorly of him.

"He was amazing. And now he's deteriorating from the inside out," I said finally. "And I don't know how to fix him. The worst part is he refuses to fix himself. He likes being punished. He thinks he deserves it."

Brooke set a contented Vicki back in my arms and I cuddled her against my cheek. Her breath was sweet with milk. "Do you think he deserves it?" Brooke asked.

I'd wasted hours mulling over how I felt about the role Nate played in Sam's death trying to figure out why he felt so responsible. For months I replayed the events of that night over and over again in my head but knew I would never see it from Nate's point of view. Only Nate and Sam knew exactly how it all went down.

Chapter Eight
Fall Semester – Second Year

The police siren was faint over the techno music blaring from the first floor of the Sigma Pi house. Lesley was dancing provocatively across the room with a guy she knew from biology class while I stood against the wall with our friend Kara nursing my warm beer.

"Where's Nate?" she asked. "He never misses a Friday night."

I shrugged my shoulders. "He had a bad practice and went home. They have a game tomorrow so I guess he's just resting up."

"They have rules about partying during the season, right?"

"Right," I acknowledged. The team had a strict no drinking policy before games which Nate took very seriously. Even still, it wasn't like him to miss out on a good time. I couldn't imagine what had happened that had him in such a funk.

Worrying about him was keeping me from enjoying myself but I couldn't help it. Part of me wanted to ditch the party and head over to his place with a movie and a bag of chips, but it seemed clear that he wanted time alone, so I stayed put. I was just about to join Lesley on the makeshift dance floor in the center of the room when I noticed flashing lights out the front window.

"I think there's something going on out there," I said to Kara, handing her my cup. "I'm gonna go see what it is."

"It's probably just that homeless guy they keep arresting for exposing himself," she called after me.

"No." I took a step closer to the window to get a better view. "There are a bunch of police cars down at the corner. And an ambulance. I'm gonna head outside to see what's going on."

The hypnotic bass of the party subsided as I made my way down the sidewalk toward the flashing lights and commotion at the end of the block. I stopped walking the moment I recognized the black pickup, its front end wrapped around the large sycamore beyond the gully on the edge of the road.

The UVA football sticker on the tailgate and chrome hubcaps meant only one thing.

The truck belonged to Sam.

I began moving again before I had a chance to process the scene before me. I had to know if he was in the truck. I had to know if Nate was with him.

"You can't get through here, Miss," someone shouted as I wove my way between the emergency vehicles.

I ignored him and continued toward the wreckage. The air was pungent with the smell of gasoline. I stood on my tip toes, craning my neck to see beyond the fireman wrestling with the jaws-of-life to free the driver, whose darkened figure I could just make out when the pulse of the red and blue police lights illuminated his face.

It was Sam.

"Sam!" I cried to the fireman. "His name is Sam! Please, please get him out!"

I began shaking, unable to control the fear that was quickly spreading through my body.

"Nate?" I called into the night to whoever was listening. "Nate!"

A pair of arms drew me into their embrace. For an instant, there was a pang of relief. He was there. He was fine.

"Miss, you can't be this close to the scene. You need to move back," the voice above me said. I looked into the face of the bystander who had warned me to stop only moments before.

I burst into tears despite my best efforts to hold myself together.

"My friend Sam is the driver," I explained between sobs. "And I'm afraid my boyfriend Nate might be with him."

The man shook his head. "I saw the whole thing happen from across the street. I was out on my porch having a smoke when the kid hit the tree. I called in the accident and was the first to respond. There was no one else in the car. Just the one fatality."

My breath hitched on the word fatality. Why would he use that word? Fatality meant dead, and smart, charismatic, college quarterbacks didn't die. They couldn't die. It was impossible, wasn't it? Sam could not be dead.

The noxious gas fumes overtook me as I tried desperately not to be sick.

An officer approached me as I steadied myself on the hood of his police cruiser.

"My friend Sam's going to be alright?" I asked him, convinced I'd simply misunderstood.

"I'm sorry," the officer began. "I'm not at liberty to give out that information at this time." He paused to take a small notepad out of his jacket pocket. "What did you say your name was?"

"I didn't," I replied, still waiting for him to confirm Sam was alive. "It's Melody Johnson. And the driver's name is Sam. Sam Murphy." I peered around him at the wreckage as the firefighter finally loosened the door from its hinges and pulled Sam's lifeless body from what remained of his truck.

I dissolved into another round of hysterics and crumpled to the ground, no longer able to support my own weight. There was only one person I could think of to talk to and I pulled my phone out of the back pocket of my jeans to dial Nate's number. He picked up on the third ring.

"Hey, Mel," he said.

"Oh my God, Nate, I'm so glad you're okay!" I wept into the receiver.

"Why wouldn't I be? I'm sitting here playing video games with Tyree."

I continued to sob, unable to speak.

"What's wrong? Why are you crying?"

I could hear the panic in his voice and took several deep breaths to compose myself. "It's Sam," I whispered.

"What about Sam? Is he with you?" His voice was thick with irritation. "Did he tell you what happened at practice? Is he still running his mouth off about how it's my fault he's getting benched tomorrow?"

"No. He didn't." I swallowed back the lump that was wedged like a rock in my throat. It was too late to keep him from the truth, and so as much as it sucked, my impulsive decision to call left me no other option than to tell him what happened. "Nate, I don't think Sam's going to be playing anymore. Maybe ever again."

"What the hell are you talking about, Mel?"

"I'm sorry. It's just, there's been an accident, and I think Sam might be dead."

Chapter Nine

Summer Break – Second to Third Year

After putting the baby down for a nap, Brooke joined me on the back porch carrying two glasses of iced tea.

"I never understood why Nate blamed himself over Sam's death. It was a DUI, wasn't it?" she asked, handing me my cup.

I set down the proposed bill I was reading and accepted the glass which was already covered in condensation from the warm air.

"Thanks," I said, waiting until she settled herself comfortably onto the wicker rocker beside me before addressing her question.

Although months had passed since the accident, it was still difficult to think about Sam, much less discuss him with another person. Talking with Brooke about his tragic death and the repercussions of his poor judgment was sure to expose my well-hidden wounds, but I'd come to accept that sharing my feelings was the only way I was ever going to heal.

"It was reported as a DUI by the police. There's a sharp curve on Virginia Avenue and apparently Sam took it too fast. Ended up crashing himself into a tree. It's a miracle he didn't hit a house. Or a person."

Brooke stirred her tea absently as she studied my face. "You never said much about it when it happened," she remarked.

It was true. In the immediate aftermath of the accident, I concentrated on putting one foot in front of the other. Nothing more. I got up. I went to class. I tried to pretend there wasn't a hole where my friend used to be. I thought I was doing the right thing. I thought I was helping by moving on.

Looking back, not sharing my anger and hopelessness was probably the worst thing I could have done. By keeping my feelings locked away, Nate assumed he was the only one still suffering.

During those months, my family hadn't pried. They hadn't forced me to rehash the accident or my sadness over losing Sam. They assumed I was going to be okay, and maybe it seemed like I was, but not because I'd truly healed. If I no longer spent my days mourning Sam it was because I filled the void created by his absence with the distraction of worrying over Nate.

Because of course Nate was filling the void with guilt and hydrocodone.

Addiction is a strange phenomenon. People can be addicted to all sorts of different things for all sorts of different reasons. There are studies which claim having an "addictive personality" is inherited. Others claim certain lifestyles promote addictive behaviors. Neither of those reasons explains why Nate abandoned reality to walk in the hazy fog of man-made opiates.

I think most of us have a point at which we just say *enough*. Perhaps we each have a predetermined level of tolerance and if your threshold is particularly high, you may never feel the need to dull the pain. But for some people there comes a time when they look to find a way out. Many choose traditional, mainstream outlets like therapy, peer mentoring, or medication. But sadly, there are those who may feel too isolated, self-conscious, embarrassed or even confused to seek professional treatment. These people often turn to mind-altering chemicals, or in the most severe instances, contemplate suicide as a way to dull the pain.

I prayed Nate would never reach that point.

I considered Brooke's astute observation that Nate did in fact blame himself for Sam's death. It seemed ridiculous that someone could blame himself for another person's stupid decision, but he did.

I took a sip of my tea and set my glass beside my binder on the porch floor. Brooke was waiting patiently for me to respond. I knew I could continue to sit in silence for the remainder of the afternoon and she wouldn't be upset. She of all people knew there were topics that were difficult to discuss.

I cleared my throat. I didn't know why.

"I didn't talk much about the accident because I didn't realize there was anything to discuss. Sam died. And it was a senseless tragedy which could have been easily avoided. He got in a car and drove after drinking God only knows how many beers. People tried to stop him, but he assured everyone he was okay."

"Was Nate one of the ones who tried to stop him?"

"No. They weren't together before the accident. They had a fight earlier in the evening and went their separate ways. Apparently, Sam was really pissed at Nate."

I watched a hummingbird hover above the feeder hanging from a hook in Brooke's garden. Surrounded by flowers full of nectar, the bird chose the ease of artificial nourishment over the more difficult task of extracting sustenance from the blossoms.

Were all creatures predisposed to take the path of least resistance?

I refocused my attention back to Brooke.

"Since Nate refuses to talk to me about it, most of what I know regarding what happened between them came from other members of the team. According to the guys, things hadn't been going well for the team during the pre-season. I think the whole mess started when a bunch of us went swimming at the quarry last summer. Sam slipped on some wet rocks and landed on his wrist, but instead of going to the doctor, he just figured it would heal on its own. I guess he didn't know how bad it was until he got back out on the field and had trouble throwing. My friend Josh told me during that first week back, Sam and Nate didn't connect on a single pass. It was like they'd never played together before.

"And tempers flared," Brooke interjected.

"Yeah. Sort of. But it gets worse. By week two, the coach realized Sam was hurt and started running practices with Zach Barnes, the backup quarterback. In the days leading up to the opening game against Ohio State, he and Nate ran every play together."

Brooke shook her head. "Let me guess. They were amazing."

"Josh said Nate caught every pass."

I remembered how he was before Sam's death. Driven. Determined. He didn't know how to not give life every bit of himself. I wondered whether he would have been willing to drop any of those passes if he'd known what the coach was going to do.

"And that made Sam angry? It wasn't Nate's fault Sam was hurt."

"I don't know for sure. I have a feeling he was angrier about what happened next."

"Which was?"

Would Sam have still been alive if Coach Anderson hadn't done what he did? Would he have gone on his post-practice binge?

Would Nate still be blaming himself?

"He benched Sam. Gave Zach, the second-string quarterback, the nationally televised showcase game against Ohio."

"Ouch."

"I know. I can't imagine how upset Sam was. Tyree told me that after practice Sam went after Nate and Zach in the locker room and accused them of making him look bad. Then he cornered Nate and told him getting benched was his fault because he hadn't caught any of his passes all week. The last thing Sam yelled before storming through the door was that he was never going to forgive Nate for losing him the showcase."

Understanding washed over Brooke's face. "Oh, Mel," she said.

It felt liberating to share the burden of Nate's story with someone other than those who were involved. It had been many months since we'd consoled one another even though we were all still very much in need of consolation.

"Now you know why I can't be mad at him for reacting like he did. He carries that accusation around with him every day. Along with the blame for the decisions Sam made that night. He believes with every bit of his soul that it's his fault that Sam died."

Anger crimsoned her cheeks. "But it's not. Sam had a choice. He chose to be reckless and stupid. He chose to put himself in a situation that led to a catastrophe." She paused. "No one made him get into that car."

I shrugged my shoulders. "I've told him that a hundred times. He doesn't listen. He doesn't *want* to listen."

Brooke leaned back and rocked methodically in her chair. The air was growing warmer and the sun threatened to break the tree line as it began its descent in the pale afternoon sky.

"He's self-medicating. Trying to deal with the guilt on his own."

It was hard thinking of the Nate I used to know as someone who could ever be depressed.

"I suppose. The worst part is I could love him in spite of his depression. I could even kind of understand why he thinks he needs the pills. But since the lying and the deception of the addiction started taking over, I just can't be around him. He's difficult to talk to and impossible to reason with. It's like I don't even know him anymore."

"Maybe I should talk to him," she mused. "Tell him about Branson."

It was just like Brooke to want to try to find a solution to the problem. It wasn't only what she did, it was who she was. Sadly, I knew Nate's addiction had grown beyond the stage where mere conversation would return him to me.

And although I hated to admit it, I knew there was always the possibility I had already lost him for good.

Chapter Ten

Fall Semester – Second Year

Nate's hand rested on my knee and he stared blankly at the watercolor reproduction hanging on the stark white wall of the ER waiting room. He hadn't spoken since picking me up in the middle of Virginia Avenue, just minutes after Sam was carried away in the ambulance. Instead, he'd been content to listen to me exhaustively rehashing the night's events.

"Do you think they're ever going to tell us anything?" I wondered aloud. "I would bet no, especially since we're not family. But what about his parents? Do you think they've been called? If the police called them when it happened, I'd think they'd be here soon."

Nate didn't respond to my series of rhetorical questions, and I glanced again at the emergency room entrance, watching for Sam's parents to burst through the doors.

Frustrated with the lack of communication regarding Sam's condition, I could no longer control my nervous energy and began pacing the room. Nate remained frozen in his chair while I milled around admissions, hoping to overhear something that would give an indication as to whether our friend had survived the crash. Of course, there was nothing to be heard.

I headed back toward the empty chair beside Nate, but the room was stifling, bordering on claustrophobic. It was the waiting, the not knowing, that forced me out of the hospital into the refuge of the parking lot and the muggy night air.

Leaning against the hospital's brick exterior, I slid my phone from my pocket and called the only person I knew would help settle my nerves.

Charlie answered on the fourth ring.

"Mel? It's late. Is everything okay?"

"I'm fine," I replied, attempting to keep the hysteria out of my voice. "But there's been an accident and my friend Sam was taken to the hospital. A guy who saw the crash told me he was dead, but the police wouldn't tell me anything at the scene, and now I'm at the hospital and the nurses aren't talking either. Nate's gone catatonic and I'm trying not to freak out. I just needed to unload and didn't know who else to call."

"Wait. Were you in the car?" I could tell he was trying to remain calm but he couldn't contain his panicked tone.

"No," I assured him, catching my breath. "But I was nearby where it happened and saw the firemen pull him out of his truck. It was really bad, Charlie. If he wasn't dead, he was definitely unconscious. I'm hoping someone's called his parents so I don't have to. I don't think I have the strength to have that conversation."

Charlie didn't respond immediately, but I heard him breathing quietly into the phone.

"I'm really glad you weren't in the accident," he said finally. "And if Sam doesn't make it, it's going to be hard, but you will get through this. Okay?"

I closed my eyes. What would I do if Sam was dead? I'd lived through my father's death and knew I could live through the death of a friend, but that didn't mean it wouldn't be painful.

"Okay," I told him, although I wondered just how long it would take to be 'okay' again.

Across the parking lot I saw two figures running toward the emergency room entrance. As they approached the front door and were illuminated by the nearby streetlights, I recognized them as Sam's parents. I quickly hung up and followed them into the hospital.

Within ten minutes a weary looking doctor arrived to share the truth of Sam's fate. His father cried out in anguish as his mother crumbled to the floor. While I joined in their grieving, murmuring words of consolation and concern, Nate stood to the side, motionless and mute. He didn't move from the corner of the empty triage room, his eyes fixed on the laces of his shoes.

We stayed at the hospital with Sam's parents for quite a while, and I continued to mourn with them as they held each other up. When a hospice nurse arrived to take them back to see the body, we realized there was no reason left to stay, and Nate and I shuffled outside to the car. Without knowing where else to go or what else to do, he drove us to his apartment where we curled up in bed together without taking the time to change out of our clothes. He turned away from me, refusing to let me look into his face, so I held him until the tightness in his muscles released and he finally fell asleep.

And then, in the quiet stillness of the early morning, I wept alone for the loss of my friend.

Word spread quickly about Sam's death thanks in no small part to the feeding frenzy of media coverage surrounding Saturday's nationally televised game, which went on as scheduled despite objections from most of the team. They trudged out onto the field wearing hastily tied black ribbons pinned to their jerseys and watched with bloodshot eyes as the coach gave an impassioned speech just before kickoff on the stadium's big screen. Kara, Lesley, and I sat in our usual section, fists full of wadded up tissues, as Nate and the others struggled against their opponents, barely going through the motions.

Although we lost spectacularly, the worst part of the game wasn't our team's performance. It was the audacity of the reporters and news media, circling like vultures, giddy with a twisted excitement about the bonus coverage surrounding the tragic death of our team's starting quarterback the night before. They buzzed around the stadium, searching for soundbites from the student body, parents, and faculty about "the horrors of college binge drinking." It was all I could do not to lash out when the perky brunette from ESPN cornered me outside the locker room while I was waiting for Nate to emerge.

"Pull the frame back a bit and let's bring the boom a little closer," she instructed her cameraman as she approached. Then she turned on the sweetness, feigning concern for my loss.

"Did you know the deceased, Sam Murphy?" she asked me, brows furrowed, head tipped to the side.

"Yes," I replied, turning my shoulder to convey I had no interest in speaking with her.

"And were you aware he had a problem with alcohol?"

I set my jaw and ignored her, my eyes set on the locker room door.

"Do you think the team was aware of his issues?" she continued, addressing Kara who was barely holding herself together.

"He didn't have any issues!" Kara spat at the reporter. "He was just upset. He made a mistake. He was an amazing quarterback and a terrific guy. It was an honor to call him my friend," she concluded, taking me by the hand to guide us out of the stadium and away from the madness.

In the days that followed, Nate and I existed in a hazy fog, both of us moving in slow motion – our only goals were to make it through the next minute, hour, sleepless night. I was the one who made arrangements for our trip to Sam's hometown where the viewing and funeral would take place while Nate was content to stay in bed.

"Sam's father called to ask if you would be a pall bearer," I said when I discovered him in his bedroom, prostrate under a blanket Monday afternoon. I waited for him to reply, but instead of a response, all I got was a grunt.

I threw the covers back and poked at him with a lacrosse stick I picked up off the floor. "We need to leave in an hour if we're going to make it to the viewing by six. I got us a hotel room so we don't have to drive back for the funeral tomorrow morning. Sam's parents offered to let us stay with them, but I didn't think you'd want to do that so I told them we already had a place." I paused, waiting for him to acknowledge me, but he simply rolled over, burying his head beneath his arm.

"Nate," I said, sitting on the bed beside him. "Talk to me."

"There's nothing to say," he murmured. "I'll get ready. I just want to be alone right now."

And so I left him alone.

I left him alone during Sam's funeral where he carried his best friend's body down the aisle in a mahogany box. I left him alone when we returned to school. And by the end of the week I could already feel the subtle shift in my relationship with Nate.

Chapter Eleven

Spring Semester – First Year

I reread the same sentence for the tenth time. My vision glazed and the words became a blurry mass of unrecognizable symbols on the screen before me. My fingers tapped impatiently on the keyboard, and as I willed them to type something coherent, I glanced at the lower right-hand corner of the screen to peek at the clock. I was hoping it was getting close to noon so I could legitimately excuse myself from my self-imposed confinement for lunch.

It wasn't even nine o'clock and I was over it. I yawned, stretched, and reworked my hair into its disheveled ponytail. After working on my sociology paper for the better part of a week, I was close to finishing, but a reasonable conclusion eluded me. I was just about to return to the computer when I heard the first tap.

It was a cracking sound. Tiny and without a definite origin.

"Did you hear that?" I whispered to Lesley, who I assumed was still asleep, curled up beneath her down comforter on the top bunk. "Les?" I called again.

She groaned loudly and rolled to face where I was now standing in the center of the room.

"What?" she asked, unable to mask the irritation in her voice.

"Did you hear that noise?"

"What kind of noise?"

"I don't know. Like a weird tap."

Just as she was about to respond, I heard it again.

"There it was!" I cried. "Did you hear it that time?"

"Yeah," she said, rising from the bed. "It almost sounded like it was outside."

I disagreed. "No, it was definitely here in the room." I cringed at the thought of what was making the sound. "I hope we don't have a mouse."

By the time we heard the noise a third time, I realized Lesley was right. I hurried toward the window to peer out into the crisp, spring morning.

Below me, smiling brightly, was Nate. I fumbled with the ancient window locks and wrestled open the sash.

"What are you doing?" I called down to him.

"Trying to get your attention," he replied, holding up the fistful of pebbles in his hand.

I shook my head at his childlike behavior. "Why not just text me, silly?"

"Texting just seemed an awfully conventional way to start the very unconventional day I have planned for us." He was beaming at me.

I imagined I could hear my unfinished paper heckling me from the computer screen.

"What kind of day do you have planned?" I asked, resting my elbows on the sill so I could lean my head out the window.

"I can't tell you. It's a surprise, but I need you to get ready fast because we need to get where we're going by ten. You need to dress warm and comfortably. Can you be ready in twenty minutes?"

My paper taunted me. I knew I needed to finish.

But life wasn't all about work.

"Yes," I replied.

"Awesome. Hurry up. I'll wait here." He blew me a kiss and made himself comfortable on the stoop.

Lesley raised an eyebrow at me as I latched the window shut and hurled myself across the room toward my closet.

"What was that all about?"

"Nate's taking me somewhere. We have to leave in twenty minutes," I replied as I stripped off my oversized t-shirt and replaced it with a tank top and hoodie.

"What about the paper you got up early to finish?" she teased.

I glared at her. "It can wait. I still have all day tomorrow to finish," I said, justifying my decision to blow off my scholarly obligation in favor of spending the day with Nate.

In less than fifteen minutes I was dressed and ready to go.

"Have fun," she called after me as I breezed out the door.

I found Nate still sitting on the front steps of the building, looking quite pleased with himself.

"Hey, Mel." He rose from the stoop, towering above me like an oak, and reached out to take my hand. For months I tried in vain to weave our fingers together as I'd done with prior boyfriends, but eventually came to realize his were simply too thick to fit comfortably between my tiny fingers. Now, my entire hand fit snugly inside of his as he swung my arm playfully at his side. I always felt safe beside him. Protected from the evils of the world. Surely no harm could come to someone so formidable.

"So where are we going?" I asked finally as we approached the parking lot where his car waited.

He pressed the button on his key fob to unlock the doors. "I'm not going to tell you," he replied.

I continued giving him the third degree as we slid into our seats and headed off Grounds. Within five minutes we were on I-64 heading east out of town.

"My only point," I persisted, "is that you can't know if I'm going to like something unless you tell me what it is in advance that we are going to do. So to that end, you should just tell me what it is that we are doing."

He remained stoic behind the wheel, unwavering in his stubborn insistence that our destination remain a surprise. "Your Jedi mind tricks won't work on me." He took his eyes from the road to risk a sideways glance in my direction.

I made no excuses for my dislike of surprises. My life had been full of unpleasant ones and I was always wary of the unknown. "Pleeeeeease," I begged.

"This is really driving you crazy, isn't it?" he laughed.

"Yes!" I exclaimed, reaching across the console to grab his bicep with both hands and shaking it with all my might. "Tell me, tell me, tell me!"

"In due time, my child," he teased. "I promise though, you'll like it."

I pretended to pout as we continued toward whatever exciting adventure awaited us. Although I protested loudly when faced with the unknown, I was getting used to Nate's fly-by-the-seat-of-your-pants approach to life which was so different from the environment I'd grown up in.

****

From the time I was a baby, my days had been structured, full of purpose and discipline. I'd been a serious child who concentrated solely on the things my parents thought were important. Good grades. Clean room. Tidy appearance. I worked diligently to ensure their happiness which wasn't difficult since I always knew what was coming next.

The predictability of my life was both a comfort and a bore. Charlie and I attended the same private school from pre-K through twelfth grade with the same children and the same daily routines. There were never any unplanned family vacations or spontaneous decisions. Every part of my life was carefully choreographed by my father so we could be the family the world expected us to be. Such was the life of a politician's daughter.

After my dad died, the pendulum of my existence swung to the opposite end of the spectrum, and I lost sight of everything he valued to focus instead on fun. His death brought unexpected chaos into our lives. One minute we were Senator Phil Johnson's Family and the next we were just The Johnsons. Faced with an identity crisis, my mother, Charlie and I went into a state of flux. We were allowed freedoms we'd never experienced before and it was a strange and wondrous thing. Out from beneath my father's thumb, Charlie used the opportunity to explore the truth of his adoption and found many secrets hidden in our family's proverbial closet. He made mistakes, large and small.

But then again, so did I.

Without my father's reins to guide her every move, my mom enjoyed a sort of renaissance. It wasn't that she didn't miss my dad, but she allowed herself to do the things she hadn't been permitted to do when she was the senator's wife. She went out without makeup. She wore sweats to the grocery store. She ate cereal for dinner and stopped apologizing for things that were out of her control. She started taking photography classes at the community college and joined a group of bird watchers on the weekends to hunt for warblers and owls. She was never at home, always off on an adventure or social outing with a stream of new friends or long forgotten ones. My mom thrived in her new reality and assumed I would blossom just as beautifully on my own without her constant supervision.

Unfortunately, this was not the case.

Charlie's companionship helped me to navigate my path in the immediate aftermath of dad's death, but when he eventually accepted an internship in Washington DC after graduation, I found myself untethered in a world in which I had always been chained to an attentive warden. My mom was never around, off exploring her own pursuits and I felt abandoned and alone. For the first time in my life, I was left to my own devices.

Around the same time, I became aware of the depth of my father's transgressions. After taking my grandmother to a doctor's appointment on our side of town, my mom brought her back to our house for lunch. The three of us ate together, but I excused myself soon after finishing so I could return to the final chapters of my overdue library book. From the next room I couldn't help but listen in on their conversation, and my ears piqued when my grandmother commented on my father's "indiscretions."

"I still can't believe he lied to you for all those years, leading you to believe adopting Charlie was an act of mercy when all along he was just covering up his own mistakes."

"Charlie wasn't a mistake, Mom," my mother replied. "I have to believe there's a reason why I was allowed to be the one to raise him. He's as good for me as I am for him. Especially now that we both know the truth."

"The truth about what a monster his father was."

Instead of a reply, I heard only the telltale clanking of dishes being piled on top of one another as Mom cleared the table. Finally, she spoke in a voice that betrayed her true feelings.

"Please, Mom. He's gone. Don't speak ill of the dead."

Grandma laughed in a way that made the hair on my arms stand on end. "Oh, I'll speak ill, alright. I can't believe after all he did that you continue to defend him."

The dishwasher door slammed shut, rattling the silverware inside.

"I'm not defending him, Mother! I'm as upset about it as you are. Even more so. But what am I to do about it now? My marriage was built on a lie. My husband used a woman to win an election, got her pregnant, and fooled me into raising his illegitimate son." Her voice rose to a frenzied pitch and, realizing her mistake, she lowered it again to just above a whisper. I strained to hear the rest of the conversation.

"It does me no good to dwell in the past. Regardless of how it happened and despite his shortcomings as a man, Phil blessed my life with two beautiful children. Charlie is still my son and he will always be my son. The bottom line is that the joy he and Melody have given me far outweigh the pain of Phil's betrayal. I've come to terms with that and I've found peace. I wish to God you would just let this go." She sighed heavily and I heard the kitchen chair creak beneath her weight as she returned to her seat at the table. "Please."

"I just feel so awful for you, but I will try."

When neither spoke for several minutes, I escaped unnoticed to my bedroom. Fueled by the truth, hidden no longer, a small ember of anger which had been smoldering since my father's passing began to burn in earnest.

Even when he traveled to DC, my father always kept close tabs on his perfect nuclear family. There was a code of conduct we were to abide by and a standard of behavior and dress we were required to maintain. It was expected that we would excel at academics and participate as civic leaders, even if it was only just for show. When he died, all of those expectations suddenly fell away, and we were released from our proverbial cage.

While my mom enjoyed her new life full of freedom and ambition, I stayed behind, struggling to come to terms with the truth about my dad. When I finally unstuck myself and consciously rejoined the world, I spent my sophomore year of high school exploring the facets of life I hadn't even known existed while he was alive. With Mom off pursuing her own agenda, there was no one checking to be sure I was completing homework assignments or studying or attending classes.

So, I simply stopped, because for the first time in my life, I could.

I only did things that made me happy, or at least things I thought would make me happy. I neglected schoolwork and healthy relationships and my responsibilities. I started drinking. Smoking pot. I found myself partying with new friends in the middle of the night, scurrying like field mice out basement windows and back doors when police arrived. There were keggers. There were benders.

And all the while, there was the fear that no one cared.

When my grades started to reflect my new lifestyle, mom realized that maybe freedom at fifteen looked entirely different from freedom at forty-seven. That perhaps I wasn't ready to make decisions for myself. At least not the big ones.

Outwardly, I fought her attempts to rein me in. When she reinstated my father's rules about curfews and mandatory homework checks, I blew up at her. I cursed. I slammed doors and threw dishes at her head. I complained to anyone who would listen about how unfairly I was being treated and how difficult my life had become. And I continued to do exactly what I wanted to do when I wanted to do it. My mom was at her wits end.

And then one day, Charlie came home.

The birds were just waking up when I stumbled through the porch slider the Saturday morning before Easter. He was there, asleep on the family room sectional with a knitted afghan across his legs and a book fanned open on his chest. In my inebriated state his presence took me by surprise and I cried out, thinking he was an intruder.

"Melody? Is that you?" he called into the dim light of morning.

I froze in place. "Yes," I replied.

He hesitated, waiting for me to acknowledge why he was there. His features were indistinguishable but I was keenly aware that he knew where I'd been and what I was doing. My soul bore the weight of his disappointment without him uttering another word.

"Charlie," I whispered at last, "I'm so sorry."

Graciously, my brother made arrangements with his job to work remotely until the end of the school year so he could be more present in my life. He blamed himself unnecessarily for my behavior, which pained me to no end. I knew I'd been acting like a spoiled brat and couldn't bear the thought of disappointing him further. He was unable to mask his displeasure and regret when I approached him with my third quarter grades. And although my GPA had plummeted to abysmal lows, he assured me that all was not lost as he cheerfully sat in on my teacher conference to discuss what could be done.

With his help and the assistance of a tutor, I was able to finish out my sophomore year with a passing average. I made amends with the old friends I'd forsaken who mercifully accepted me back into their fold.

Most importantly, I confided in Charlie about the conversation I overheard concerning my dad, and when I told him what I'd discovered, he broke down in tears.

"I never wanted to keep secrets from you, Mel," he said. "I know what it means to be lied to, but I couldn't stand the thought of being the one to taint your memories of him. I didn't have it in me I guess. Please don't be angry."

He was easily forgiven since there was no doubt in my mind that his intentions were pure. With my mom's approval, he encouraged me to resume the weekly appointments with Dr. Richmond I'd abandoned in exchange for my path of destruction. He helped me to explore my feelings regarding my father, and discussed why I acted out instead of choosing a healthier outlet for my pain and confusion. After several weeks, the raging fire inside me was reduced to smoldering ashes.

Back on the straight and narrow, I became my own parole officer and task master, resolved to graduate with a respectable average. I focused solely on schoolwork for the remainder of my high school career, neglecting most friendships and would-be suitors. I was determined not to let a season of poor decisions keep me from my life's goals. The day my acceptance letter arrived from UVA, I finally exhaled. Everything was going to be okay.

I considered myself lucky, realizing the error of my ways before destroying my life. Unfortunately, instead of solving my problems by finding balance between the two worlds, I'd simply reverted back to what I knew.

Structure. Order. Routine.

And then, as fate would have it, Nate walked into my life before classes even began, testing the limits of my firmly established boundaries. He'd been testing them ever since.

Chapter Twelve

Spring Semester – First Year

Nate pulled the car onto a gravel drive in an unfamiliar area off the interstate. There was a large sign at the entrance to the road that read "VSA."

"We're here!" he announced, the air around him pulsing with excitement.

"Fabulous," I said dryly, making a great show of rolling my eyes as he pulled in front of a large building which appeared to be some sort of hangar. "If only I knew where 'here' was."

After parking the car, Nate glanced nervously at his watch and then at me. "We only have a couple minutes until our scheduled time. Now if you're scared or don't want to do it, I completely understand and I won't be upset. I promise. But I want you to at least take the preparation class and see what you think at the end before you make your final decision, okay?"

I was beginning to wonder if he was losing his mind. Had he forgotten that I still had no idea where we were or what we were doing?

"I'd be happy to make a decision if you would share with me what we're doing here! Is this some kind of airport?"

"Yeah. Sort of." He unbuckled his seatbelt and stepped outside, but when I didn't follow him, he leaned back in to encourage me out of the car. "Come on. They're waiting for us."

As exasperated as I was curious, I trailed behind him into the hangar where there were a handful of men milling about. One of them turned to greet us as we entered.

"You must be Nate," he called, crossing the expanse in great strides. "I'm glad you found us! I'm Paul. We spoke on the phone last week."

"Oh, hey," Nate replied, taking his hand, "it's nice to meet you."

"And this," he said, turning to me, "must be Melody. It's nice to meet you too."

Paul appeared to be in his mid-forties and was at least as big as Nate, if not bigger. He looked down at me with the mischievous grin of a schoolboy. His handshake was painfully firm and I was glad when he released his grip and returned his attention to Nate.

"Are you guys ready to get started?"

I glared up at Nate and crossed my arms across my chest. I was done being kept in the dark. Enough was enough.

"Get started with what?" I asked.

A deliberate look passed between Paul and Nate.

"You decided to keep it a secret after all," Paul laughed, nudging Nate playfully on the shoulder. "That was a bold move."

Nate tousled my hair as if I was a golden retriever. "She can handle it. She loves surprises."

I threw his hand off my head and grabbed the front of his shirt. I was losing my patience and my sense of humor.

"Just tell me what we're doing, Nate, or so help me, I will..."

"We're going skydiving," he interrupted. "I thought for sure you'd have figured it out by now."

I suddenly noticed the rigging two of the men were assembling on a table in the far corner of the room. Behind them, hanging on the wall, were bright purple jumpsuits and half a dozen posters of reckless thrill-seekers plummeting to the earth. How had I missed seeing them?

As I finally processed what was going on, part of me was thrilled.

And the other part was petrified.

"Skydiving?" I stammered. "Like with a parachute? Out of a plane? From up in the air?"

Both men chuckled good-naturedly at my ridiculous litany of questions.

"Yes," Paul said, pulling me into the crook of his arm to lead me further into the hangar, "like with a parachute. I don't think any of us want to try it without one."

I looked over my shoulder at Nate who was following behind. I could tell by the look on his face he was nervous about whether or not I was going to join him on his adventure. He gave me a thumbs-up and mouthed the words 'I love you' as Paul began filling us in on what we would experience during our hour together.

My head began to spin as the three of us sat at a table at the far end of the hangar. Paul, who I learned would be our instructor as well as Nate's tandem jumper, spent the next twenty minutes explaining to us what would take place during the jump. I zoned out repeatedly as he talked about harness fittings and wind speeds. At some point, Nate took my hand and wrapped it inside his. I knew he was trying to put me at ease, but as the minutes ticked past, my anxiety grew. We watched a short video about how the company and its agents would not be held legally accountable for any injury or loss sustained as a result of the activity and then he presented us with paperwork to sign.

As I read the clause about death, I thought of my dad who died senselessly on a rock climbing expedition when his harness gave way. I reminded myself that he had been murdered. People jumped out of perfectly good planes all the time. Nate wouldn't ask me to do anything that wasn't safe.

I would be fine.

I steadied my hand to sign my name at the bottom of the form.

"You're going with me then?" Nate whispered into my ear.

"I guess so," I replied, my voice wavering slightly. "I can't let you have all the fun."

As we sat beside one another during the seventeen-minute plane ride, Nate nervously tugged at his fittings. It was unlike him to worry over anything, and it was nice to see that he was human after all. I sidled up close beside him so he could hear me over the hum of the plane's engines.

"Thank you," I said.

He stopped fidgeting and tucked a loose strand of hair behind my ear. "You're welcome," he replied.

"This had to have cost you a fortune. I hope you're not eating ramen all week because of me."

He shook his head and traced the outline of the patch on the shoulder of my jumpsuit. "I actually got the passes from my brother. He won two tandem jumps at a charity auction at work, and since Laura's pregnant, they couldn't go. He offered them to me over Christmas break and I've been waiting for it to warm up to take you ever since."

His generosity and thoughtfulness warmed my heart and took my mind off the fact that his idea of a romantic date involved possible death. I couldn't believe he'd kept it a secret for so many months.

"Thanks for taking me instead of Tyree," I told him, as our instructors motioned for us to slide down the bench toward the door.

"I told you the day I met you I was your guy if you were looking for fun. I'm just trying not to disappoint."

"You never disappoint," I assured him. I kissed him gently on the lips and was surprised when my lips were met with an atypical sense of desperation. I realized instantly that he was more anxious about the jump than he was letting on. "That was for luck. I'll see you on the ground."

He hesitated, looking me in the eyes. "Love you," he said.

"Love you back," I replied.

We strapped onto our partners and before I had a chance to reconsider the foolishness of what I was about to do, I was out of the plane.

My fall from thirteen thousand feet was life-affirming. People use that phrase a lot when they really mean that an experience was important or memorable.

For me, it was truly a spiritual event.

Before leaving the world behind and then rushing back to meet it at one-hundred-twenty miles per hour, I'd always lived my life in extremes – all business or all pleasure, never a mixture of both.

As the earth raced toward me, I saw with sudden clarity how beautiful life could be when a sense of balance is maintained. Things didn't have to be all one way or the other. I could be the best version of myself while still enjoying life's pleasures.

I could work hard to get good grades and risk my life skydiving at the same time.

Nate touched down with his partner on a grassy patch not far from where I landed and once he was released from his restraints, he ran to embrace me.

"So, what'd you think?" he asked breathlessly, nuzzling his face against the top of my head.

Although I really wanted to thank him for helping me to see the importance of maintaining balance in my life, thriving in the vibrant colors instead of existing in the black and white, I decided to keep it simple.

"I thought it was amazing," I told him. "Just like you."

Chapter Thirteen

Fall Semester – Second Year

Less than two weeks after Sam's death the world expected us to return to our classes and practices and lives as if nothing had happened. But something had happened. And I watched as those of us in Sam's inner circle who were most affected by his absence dealt with our grief in very different ways.

Mild-mannered Josh metamorphosized into the Incredible Hulk. To say he was angry was an understatement. He threw his backpack across our stats class when he couldn't find his assignment and kicked a trashcan over in the dining hall when they didn't have his favorite cereal. As he lashed out at innocent bystanders across campus, I knew the person he was really angry with was Sam, but of course Sam wasn't available to receive the brunt of his fury.

Kara wept. And wept. She couldn't make it through meals or her classes or even movie night without having to excuse herself to the restroom, where she would cry and reapply her mascara, as if her shaky composure wasn't enough to give her emotional instability away.

Known for being the strong, silent type, suddenly Tyree wouldn't shut up. He droned on endlessly while we played video games about honoring Sam and his life with our words and our actions. About making his life "mean something" so Sam's death wouldn't be "in vain." He began working to set up a scholarship foundation in

Sam's honor and started a petition to have his jersey number retired. Tyree was a force of nature.

Lesley was her typical moody self. She moped around and threw visual daggers at anyone who crossed her. The change in her demeanor after the accident was subtle, but it was there. I caught her staring at a picture of her and Sam together on her phone and wasn't surprised when she snapped at me to leave her alone when she realized I was watching.

For my part, I did what I always did, which amounted to throwing myself into my schoolwork and taking comfort in the things I could control, like completing assignments and showing up to debate team. And while I didn't understand my friends' reactions, it was comforting to know they were working through their pain in their own way just like I was.

And then there was Nate.

He didn't react to Sam's death using any of the coping mechanisms the rest of us subscribed to. There was no anger or aggression. No crying or call to make the world a better place.

He just checked out. Of everything.

"We're all going out for burgers. You coming?" I asked, tossing his jacket beside him on the sofa where he spent most of his waking hours.

He didn't look away from the TV. "No."

"No?" I said, shoving his legs to the side so I could sit down on the couch. "Why not?"

His eyes flicked in my direction. "Because I don't *want* to go out for burgers."

I punched him playfully on the arm. "You love burgers," I said. "Burgers are your favorite. In fact... wait! Do you hear that? I think it's a burger calling your name!! 'Nate! Come eat me!'" I called.

He turned his attention back to the TV. "I'm not going, Mel. You're welcome to head out though. Don't let me stop you."

I tried not to be disappointed as he used the remote to scroll through talk shows and news stations. "I'm not going out alone again. I went to the concert without you last night and it sucked. I just miss hanging out, Nate." I slid my feet under his legs and shrugged out of my fleece. "We can just stay here together and veg out. I'll fix us grilled cheese. How does that sound?"

He didn't respond but I felt the need to stay. I made grilled cheeses and a pattern emerged with the two of us eating homemade meals from the sofa during the weeks that followed, which enabled Nate to continue avoiding life.

Midway through football season, Coach Anderson pulled him for the last quarter of our home game against Syracuse. For the first time ever, I watched from the stands as the offense played without its first string tight end.

"Did you get hurt?" I asked when he emerged from the locker room after the game.

"No," he replied, his gear thrown over his shoulder. "I'm just exhausted. I told him to take me out because I had nothing left. This is what happens when you don't sleep."

I fell into step beside him and thrust my mittened hands deep into my coat pockets. "I thought you went to health services to see about getting something to help you?"

"I did. Weeks ago. And they gave me something. It's the only reason I've been getting any sleep at all. But when I went back for a refill on the prescription they wouldn't give me any more." His voice was harsh. Strained.

"So now you're not sleeping again?" I was outraged for him. "That's not fair. They're supposed to help you. How are you supposed to keep up with everything if you're not sleeping?"

He shrugged. "I don't know. But I can't live like this. I can't fall asleep and when I finally do, nightmares wake me up." I could tell he didn't want to talk about it any further. "I guess I'll just have to figure something out."

I suggested he cut out caffeine or try reading before bed to help him fall asleep, but he shot down all of my suggestions.

"If health services won't give me what I need, I'll get it somewhere else," he told me. "This guy from kinesiology class said he gets Adderall from a dude who lives on Tenth Street. He says I can get whatever I want from him."

I couldn't believe what I was hearing. "That's illegal," I scolded. "If someone finds out you'll get kicked off the team. Or out of school. Or arrested."

He scoffed. "If I don't get some sleep it's not gonna matter anyway. Besides, it's just sleeping pills, Mel. It's not heroin."

After our initial conversation about acquiring the pills illegally, we didn't speak about it again. I didn't bring it up because I was scared to know the truth. And when he seemed to come out of the fog just before Thanksgiving - eating meals with the rest of us, coming to parties at night, and even returning to his early morning classes, I thought perhaps he'd rounded a corner and was finally sleeping on his own. I thought perhaps he was finally going to be okay.

And then I caught him fishing through my backpack in the middle of the crowded cafeteria.

"What are you doing?" I asked when I returned to the table after grabbing a sandwich from the lunch counter.

He turned away, evasively. "Nothing. Just looking for a pen."

"A pen for what? You don't even have your books with you."

When he wouldn't face me and refused to make eye contact, I knew instinctively he was lying.

"Can't a person just borrow a pen without being given the third degree?" he snapped, pushing back from the table as he threw my backpack to the floor. "I don't need this crap from you today, Melody. Enjoy your lunch."

He stormed off, leaving a trail of astonished onlookers in his wake. His anger was excessive and unwarranted and it hurt. I sat alone at the table, embarrassed, my panini getting cold, trying to understand what was causing him to be so antagonistic. As I pondered his behavior I remembered the pile of spare change I kept in the front pocket of my bag. A stone settled in the pit of my stomach as I dug through my backpack and realized my entire stash was gone. I knew immediately Nate had taken it and that there was something more to his bad mood than just exhaustion. There was a reason he was stealing from me and the only logical explanation was for pills.

After the backpack incident, I began looking for other signs of theft. And unfortunately, I found many, one after another.

It took weeks to work up the courage to confront him about it.

"My ring is missing," I said, plopping down beside him on the sofa where he was taking a mid-morning nap.

He roused slowly, propping himself up on his elbows as he attempted to focus on my face. "Your what now?"

"My ring is missing," I repeated. "You know, the amethyst one from my grandmother?"

"So," he said, rolling his neck from side to side.

"So?" I glared at him. "So do you have any idea where it might be?"

His eyes darted nervously around the room. "How the hell should I know where your stupid ring is? It's not my job to keep track of your stuff."

I tried not to let his harsh demeanor rile me. "It's funny because my ATM card went missing for a few days too and a couple hundred dollars was withdrawn. When I changed the code the card magically reappeared on the dashboard of my car. Do you know anything about that?"

He was awake now and surprisingly lucid, glaring at me from the end of the couch. "Are you accusing me of stealing from you?"

"Are you stealing from me? You're the only one who knows my pin," I replied, fearful of the answer I might get.

"I don't need to have this conversation with you, Melody," he barked. "If you don't trust me, that's your problem, not mine." He stood up and lumbered toward the kitchen, calling out to me over his shoulder. "Is that the only reason you stopped by? To accuse me of taking your stuff?"

A tiny sliver of remorse shot through my heart. Accusing him *was* the only reason I had for stopping by, and while I'd hoped he would confess what he was doing and admit he needed help, it was clear that he had no intention of doing either of those things.

He didn't want to tell the truth. And maybe it was because, in my heart, I didn't really want to hear it.

Chapter Fourteen

Summer Break – Second to Third Year

Since the clinic's part-time veterinarian wasn't arriving until September, Brooke had no choice but to return to work full-time once her maternity leave was over. Vicki's early arrival slipped a monkey wrench into her well-laid plans, but I was able to rearrange my summer work schedule to accommodate babysitting responsibilities.

Adjusting to the daily routine of a baby was something for which I was unprepared. She cried. She ate. She slept. I changed diapers, warmed bottles, and perfected my burping technique. I learned how to strap her into her car seat without waking her up and how to swaddle her arms to her sides so she wouldn't flail uncontrollably in her sleep.

But more than anything else, I learned how easy it was to fall in love with someone I barely knew.

I arrived each morning just after eight, letting myself in through the back door into the country kitchen of the century-old farmhouse Brooke and Charlie called home. On this morning I wasted no time stealing Vicki from Brooke's arms as she poured her second cup of coffee into a travel mug, and after I kicked off my flip flops beside the door, I got to the important business of covering Vicki's cheeks with kisses.

"Good morning my little bug-a-boo," I whispered in her ear. "Did you have a good night-night?"

Brooke rolled her eyes in exasperation as she screwed the lid tightly on her cup. "I wish! She had anything *but* a good night-night, and to make matters worse, she's been uncharacteristically fussy since she woke us up for the last time just after five." She groaned dramatically before collapsing onto the bar stool, the dark circles beneath her eyes revealing the depth of her exhaustion. She laid her head on the kitchen counter and covered her head with her arms. "She had us up three times last night squirming in her crib like it was the middle of the day. I swaddle her arms to her sides the best I can, but as soon as she wriggles them free, she's awake. And then so am I. I wouldn't trade her for the world, but good grief… I don't know how I'm going to function today."

I smiled at Vicki who was focusing intently on the sunglasses resting on top my head. I took them off to hand to her and she reflexively closed her tiny fingers around the earpiece.

"Just go to the clinic and try to concentrate the best you can. You're not doing any surgeries today, right?" I asked Brooke.

"No," she replied, still sprawled atop the counter, "just routine exams, thank goodness. The others were smart enough to know how tired new moms can be so they preemptively took over all my surgeries until fall. I didn't believe them about the fatigue before she was born." She peeked at me from beneath her elbow. "I believe them now."

I cradled the bundle of blankets in my arms, swaying her gently from side to side. "While you're gone today, I'll wear this little bunny out, won't I?" I cooed at Vicki, who was still clutching my sunglasses in her fist.

Brooke lifted her head from the counter. "I don't know how I would have made it through this summer without your help, Mel," she said. "It's been hard leaving her every day, but knowing she's with you has been such a blessing. And look how she adores you. She's going to miss you when you head back to school in a few weeks." She paused, considering me seriously from across the kitchen. "We all are."

I didn't want to think about school, especially since I'd be returning without Nate. I pushed the thought to the back of my mind and concentrated instead on the day ahead of me. Feedings. Diapers. Playtime. Naps.

Vicki blinked expectantly, her delicate lashes fluttering before her eyes, as if she presumed that I had something important to tell her. Wanting not to disappoint but having no degree in baby whispering, I decided just to wing it and hoped whatever I came up with would be enough to keep her occupied.

"We're gonna do a whole bunch of fun stuff today so you'll be all tuckered out for tonight and then your poor mom will be able to get some rest. What d'you say, Miss Vic? Are you gonna give your mom a break?"

She regarded me with a look of confusion and then, out of nowhere, her face split into an unprecedented grin, a glorious display of lips and gums. I couldn't believe it.

"Come quick!" I cried. "She's smiling at me!"

"She's what?" Brooke asked, pushing back from the counter, nearly knocking over her chair in the process.

"She's smiling," I repeated. "Come see!"

She crossed the kitchen in three strides and peered over my shoulder at Vicki who was now staring at us both as if we'd lost our minds.

"She was just doing it. Maybe I can get her to do it again, can't I Miss Vic? Are you gonna smile for your momma? Are you gonna make her happy after keeping her up all night?"

Vicki's eye lit up and tiny dimples puckered her cheeks as she smiled for a second time.

"Oh, my goodness!" Brooke exclaimed. "She's smiling! She's actually smiling! I have to run and get my phone!"

It took several moments for her to recover the missing phone from the depths of her purse, and by the time she returned to capture Vicki's deliciousness for posterity, I'd resorted to a game of peek-a-boo. It was a small price to pay for a new grin each time I peered out from behind my hands.

Brooke positioned herself beside me, firing off shot after shot of Vicki demonstrating her new skill, and I considered how becoming a parent was similar to becoming a full-fledged paparazzi. However, less than a minute later and despite the fact that Vicki continued to ham it up, the photo session came to an abrupt end as Brooke quietly slipped the phone into her pocket. She froze, tilting her head to the side to gaze wistfully at her daughter. Tears welled in her eyes.

"Charlie's gonna be so sorry he missed her first smile."

Before that instant, I had never stopped to consider the transience of firsts. There could be only one first time, and when the moment was over, it would never be again. It made me sad to think Charlie had missed this particular first.

"We don't have to tell him," I consoled her. "Maybe I can get her to do it again when he gets home from work this afternoon. I'll act like it's a surprise."

She considered my suggestion for a moment, tenderly tracing the contours of her daughter's ear with her fingertip. "Nah," she said finally, shaking her head. "We're gonna miss stuff. That's just part of being a parent. Maybe he'll catch her first giggle or her first step, but for now, I'll send him a picture of her first smile. It won't surprise him to discover that you were responsible for coaxing it out of her."

I cuddled Vicki on the family room sofa and switched on the morning news while Brooke texted half a dozen cheeky photos to Charlie. I attempted to smooth the wisps of hair sprouting from her head in every direction while she struggled to focus on my face. Her eyelids were heavy and I knew she would be ready for a bottle and a nap before long. I'd learned it was best to settle her before she became overtired and I considered whether I would have the strength to put her in her crib as I was instructed or if I would allow her to nap peacefully in my arms instead. Brooke appeared from the kitchen to kiss us both on the top of the head. We received the same send-off every day.

"I love you bunches," she said. "Take care of my little buttercup, and I'll see you tomorrow." She called goodbye as she slipped out through the door to the garage, and with that, Vicki and I were alone.

As expected, she fell asleep half-way through her morning bottle and as expected, I allowed her to nap undisturbed in my arms. Brooke warned me repeatedly against conditioning her to sleep outside her crib, but I couldn't see the harm in letting her nap where she felt safe. I flipped between talk shows and game shows on TV and finally settled on reading through some of the notes I'd taken on Senator Turner's latest campaign strategies the last time we met.

Charlie took great pleasure in giving me a hard time about my chosen career path, but deep down I knew he respected and supported my plan. Knowing firsthand the corruptive powers behind many elected officials' campaigns, Charlie chose to avoid a career in politics altogether, instead focusing on serving the public through non-profit organizations. I, on the other hand, decided to change the system from the inside by working with specific politicians who were passionate about running clean campaigns, free from mudslinging and special interest group funding. Senator JoAnne Turner, the woman elected to fill my father's seat after his death, was one of those politicians.

As a founding member of the Bipartisan Committee for Campaign Reform (BCCR), Senator Turner was instrumental in passing a series of laws effectively eliminating election funding from lobbyists. She also had her sights set on abolishing straw man fallacies from advertising campaigns and debates, especially those targeted at certain minority groups.

My left arm had fallen asleep and I carefully adjusted my position on the couch so I could use a pillow to help support Vicki's weight as she slumbered, her pacifier dangling precariously out of her mouth. I tapped it back into place and she began sucking vigorously in her sleep.

I reread Turner's Straw Man Policy which happened to be one of her many projects I found particularly interesting. Over the years she'd fought passionately for specific candidates and even entire political parties who had been demonized by fallacies in one form or another.

> *"Although 'straw manning' your opponent can be an effective debate or campaign strategy, it is undoubtedly a philosophically and intellectually dishonest approach which should be eliminated from our practice as elected officials. To misrepresent an opponent's position in a way that makes it look unreasonable with the intention of creating a straw man to be knocked down is among the lowest forms of debate and should be eliminated, regardless of whether the fallacy is unintentional or deliberate. This lowbrow strategy is often aimed at young voters as well as the elderly who may not have as robust an understanding of the topic being discussed. I propose legislation to penalize those candidates who use straw man arguments as part of their political campaigns by reducing their federal funding cap."*

I remembered an assignment in my political philosophy class in which we were each assigned a debate topic and instructed to come up with ways to undermine one another's positions. Many of my classmates opted to straw man one another because when they discovered its ability to draw on emotions, it proved to be one of the easiest solutions. My topic was the need for an increase of government assistance to the poor to offset the effects of inflation. Over half of my classmates were unable to challenge my position successfully with facts and opted instead to use straw man fallacies. Several blamed me for being a "bleeding-heart liberal." Others accused me of wanting to steal money from "hard-working" taxpayers to take care of "lazy slobs." A few even denounced my position as being nothing more than government sanctioned theft.

Needless to say, we all learned a valuable lesson about how easy it is to fall into the habit of attacking a position that's not actually held by the opposing side in the hopes of making your own position appear stronger.

I read through the proposal Turner intended on presenting to Congress in the fall. It was solid, but I knew she was up against stiff opposition. There were many incumbents in Washington who took offense to her no nonsense, take action approach to reform, but I truly believed in her agenda. I hoped my summer internship would land me a paid position on her staff at BCCR after graduation. In June, I'd been tasked with the assignment of reaching out to both retired and current congressmen and women who were sympathetic to her cause. I'd made phone calls to over a hundred individuals throughout most of the country with relative success. With my one free hand, I began consolidating a short-list of the west coast candidates who had supported her in the past to call later in the week.

Halfway through Oregon, a buzzing sound distracted me from my progress. It took me a moment to remember that I'd set my phone on vibrate so it wouldn't wake Victoria if it rang while she was napping. I quickly shuffled the paperwork from my lap to the floor and slid the sleeping bundle from my left arm onto the sofa in the space between my legs so I could reach my phone on the table behind me. I didn't recognize the number on the screen but decided to answer the call anyway.

"Hello?" I whispered into the receiver.

"Melody?"

I recognized Nate's voice at once. He sounded haggard. And scared. Panic immediately set in.

"Nate? What is it? Is something wrong?"

Three days had passed since we'd last spoken. Our conversation included a heated exchange, ending with a series of accusations and hostile declarations. I recalled the pain in his voice as he'd said goodbye.

Nate sighed deeply on the other end of the line, and I sat in transfixed anticipation of the reason for his call. Finally, he spoke.

"I'm at the police station here at home."

My mind immediately began cataloguing the numerous explanations for why he would be at the police station. None of them were good.

I couldn't bring myself to respond. He was waiting for me to ask but I wouldn't. I couldn't.

"Mel?"

"I'm here," I said.

He hesitated. His silence was rife with embarrassment.

"Whatever it is, Nate, we'll figure it out," I said in an attempt to coerce him into communicating what had happened.

I could barely make out his response. "I got arrested," he mumbled.

I closed my eyes. Steadied my breathing. Braced myself for what I knew was coming.

"Okay," I replied as calmly as I could.

"I can't call my folks." He took several deep breaths. "Can you come bail me out?"

I glanced at Vicki napping peacefully between my calves. She was my responsibility. Nate was not. And yet being present for him was the very definition of love. Love meant showing up even when you didn't want to, and in this particular instance, I really, really didn't want to.

But I had to.

"I've got the baby so I need to call Brooke to make sure it's okay if I bring her along," I snapped. "Then I have to put away what I'm doing and get all her stuff packed up. It's gonna be a while until I'll be ready to head out so you're gonna have to just sit tight."

Nate coughed several times and I could tell he was trying to hold himself together. Because that's what he did. He held it together because he thought that's what the world expected him to do.

"Thanks, Mel," he said finally.

"Don't thank me yet. I have a good mind to just leave you there and let you stew in your own mess for a while..."

"Please don't. Please come get me." He coughed again. "I need you, Mel."

I glanced at the digital clock below the TV. It was just before noon which meant if I woke Vicki she would need to be fed and changed before we left. "I'll be there in about two hours with my paycard," I said finally.

There was an awkward silence as Nate attempted to stifle his despondency. "Okay. I'll see you soon," he said at last. "I love you."

His final words tore through me. I struggled with the idea that somewhere, buried deep below the wretchedness of his addiction, a cinder of his love for me still burned.

A part of me worried that it would eventually be snuffed out.

Another part worried that it wouldn't.

Chapter Fifteen

Fall Semester-First Year

"You're gonna have to suck it up on the alumni side with us," Charlie teased as we pulled into the parking lot of Virginia Tech's Lane Stadium. "And if you're cheering for Nate too loudly, it might get ugly. I don't know if I'll be able to protect you."

I was happy to have caught a ride with Brooke and Charlie to see Nate's final game of the season against the Hokies in Blacksburg. Since they both earned their graduate degrees from Virginia Tech and were headed to the game anyway, they were happy to let me tag along, though we clearly disagreed about which team was going to win.

The temperature was only in the mid-thirties but the sun was shining, and with enough layers I was almost warm. Since most of the alumni seats were in the shade, I was glad we'd brought a pile of blankets from home. I convinced myself that freezing was a small price to pay for the chance to be closer to where Nate would be on the visiting side of the field.

Brooke stopped a dozen times to say hello to professors and students she knew on her way through the crowd, so by the time we finally got to our seats, it was almost time for the kickoff. Once we settled ourselves on the cold, metal bleachers, I was thrilled to discover we were close enough to the field to spot Nate in his position at Sam's right, toward the end of the offensive line.

Our first drive resulted in a field goal, which Tech quickly trumped with a touchdown of their own in the middle of the first quarter. The boys were down seven to three, and with the deafening Hokies crying out for defense, it seemed like I was the only person in the crowd cheering for UVA as they approached the end zone. That was until I heard Charlie shouting Nate's name when he managed a difficult first down to put UVA within field goal range.

It was amazing to watch Sam and Nate in action together on the field. Although two years his senior, Sam had immediately taken Nate under his wing at the start of the season. Their coach's unconventional strategies often connected Sam and Nate to one another on the field, and the level of camaraderie established during play quickly found its way into the boys' personal relationship, rendering them nearly inseparable. They ate meals together, hung out in each other's rooms playing videogames, went to parties together, and had even been known to wash each other's laundry. By the end of their first season together, they were more brothers than teammates and that level of trust translated seamlessly onto the field.

I held my breath as Sam rocketed the ball toward Reggie, one of his go-to wide receivers. The throw careened out of bounds and cheers erupted from the entire stadium. After a quick huddle, Sam handed off the ball to a running back everyone called Shoestring. I had no idea what his actual name was and I had no idea what his nickname meant, but when he was tackled inches from the goal line, it was Nate who helped him up off the ground.

As the team set up for what would probably be the final play of the drive, I sat on my hands, not only to keep them warm but also to prevent me from jumping out of my skin. I caught a look pass between Sam and Nate and knew instinctively that Sam was giving him the ball. As the play clock ticked down and the snap was released, Nate headed across the field behind the line of scrimmage. Sam faked a pass to the opposite side of the field, but I wasn't fooled. I knew where the ball was going. Sure enough, Sam turned in the final seconds before an impending sack and handed off the ball to Nate who ran unobstructed into the end zone for a touchdown.

Hokie groans overpowered our cheers, but as Nate approached the sidelines, he was greeted by a procession of high fives and slaps to the rear from his teammates and coaches. I watched as he turned his face toward the stands and began scanning the spectators for signs of a familiar face. I went to every home game but had never managed to attend any away games because of the distance and lack of transportation. It was a big deal for him that I'd convinced Brooke and Charlie to bring me, and I could tell by the look in his eyes he was hoping I saw his touchdown. As his gaze grew closer to where I was sitting, I began waving my hands frantically above my head in the hopes of grabbing his attention. Happily, my enthusiasm worked, and he returned my gesture by blowing a double handed kiss in my direction.

"He's really something, huh?" Charlie teased, elbowing me in the ribs in a very big-brother sort of way. "Almost like he's showing off for someone special."

"He is something," I agreed, ignoring his jabs, both physical and playful. I wouldn't allow Charlie's banter to get the better of me although I knew it was good-natured. As the only male role model in my life for so many years, he took his position of authority very seriously and was mindful of the boys I'd dated during high school. He never told me who I could and couldn't see, but he always made sure the boys knew he was around to protect me. Since Nate and I had already been together three months without a single opportunity for them to officially meet, I knew Charlie was hoping to make his presence known after the game.

"What's his major again?" he asked.

"Anatomy and physiology. He wants to be a physical therapist."

He nodded as if he had Nate all figured out, helping himself to another nacho from the plastic container we were sharing. "Gonna try and get in with an NFL team or something if he doesn't get drafted?"

"No," I replied, "I think he wants to work with the elderly. Like rehabilitative therapy."

He took his attention off the game long enough to raise an eyebrow in my direction.

"Seriously?"

I shrugged my shoulders and took a sip of my lukewarm hot chocolate. "Yeah. Seriously. His parents are really pushing for him to draft with the NFL, but he says it's not the lifestyle he's interested in living. He's good though, don't you think? I bet he'd have a shot."

Charlie nodded thoughtfully as our defense stopped the Hokies at their own forty-yard line. "Yeah. I bet he would. He's had a great season. But if it's not what he wants, no one should pressure him into it. He should make his own decisions."

"Like you made your own decision about using your trip to find your birth mother?" Now I was the one jabbing him in the ribs. "Look how great that almost turned out."

"Hey," Brooke piped up, "he may have hit a few hurdles, but things have certainly worked out for your brother. The decisions he's made have been his own. It's a gift to be able to live your life on your own terms."

I threw my hands up in my own defense. "Hey! I'm not the one shoving football down his throat. That's his family. I told you there's dozens of them, between all his brothers and sisters and their husbands and wives and kids. I think they see dollar signs when they look at Nate."

"And you don't?" Charlie asked.

I had never stopped to consider what attracted me to Nate. Our relationship was in its infancy, and the allure of financial freedom hadn't even crossed my mind. I didn't see Nate as a meal ticket or a security blanket. I saw him as a guy who enjoyed the fellowship of playing on a team with his friends and the companionship of being in a relationship with me. I hadn't thought much further than the end of the first semester and I certainly didn't harbor any delusions about becoming an NFL wife. I was with Nate because he made me laugh, he made time for me, and he made me feel appreciated. There was nothing more to it than that.

"No. Honestly, if we should end up together, like really end up together, I'd rather him be happy than rich."

Charlie blew into his hands to warm them and leaned around me to share a conspiratorial look with Brooke. "She's a good egg, this one."

"Always has been," she replied.

I rolled my eyes at how cheesy the two of them could be but secretly delighted in the warmth of my family's love as we cheered the Cavaliers to a twenty-three to seventeen victory. Sam and Nate connected for a second touchdown in the beginning of the fourth quarter and they ended up winning on field goals. I couldn't help but feel a surge of pride as we watched the team celebrate their victory from the stands above.

We waited for what seemed like hours outside the locker rooms for the team to appear. A few straggled out in twos and threes before a massive swell of unmitigated testosterone flooded through the double doors. In the center of it all were Nate and Sam, freshly showered and giddy as two schoolboys given a free pass from detention. Nate noticed me before I could call to him and he hurried to my side, planting a kiss on my cheek.

"How's my favorite cheerleader? Did you enjoy the game?"

"I did. You were amazing."

"Nah. I was just in the right place at the right time." He adjusted his duffle on his shoulder and noticed my family standing behind me. He leaned forward and extended his hand to Charlie. "Hey. I'm Nate. You must be Melody's brother, Charlie. Nice to meet you."

"Nice to meet you too, Nate. Melody's told us a lot about you." He released his hand from Nate's grip and took a step back to keep from having to crane his neck in order to see him fully. "That was one heck of a show you boys put on out there today. Great way to end the season."

"It always feels good to win," Nate agreed.

Brooke slid past me and took a step in his direction. "This is my sister-in-law, Brooke," I said, by way of introduction as Nate overpowered her with a hug she clearly wasn't expecting.

"It's a pleasure to meet you," she said from beneath the folds of his jacket.

"You too! It's nice to finally put faces to all the stories Melody's told me about you all."

Charlie rubbed the back of his neck and drew his breath in sharply. "I can only imagine what she's told you," he chuckled. "There certainly is a lot to tell!"

Our laughter was followed by uncomfortable silence, and I stared at the ground, not knowing what to say as I kicked the gravel drive with my boots. Most of the team had already boarded the bus headed back to school, and it was time for us to leave as well.

But the truth was, I didn't want him to go back.

I wanted him to come home with me.

I tucked my hair behind my ears and peered up at him. His eyes were the same color as the sky, but full of ever so much more promise. The promise of who we were together being far more amazing than who we were apart.

I couldn't stop myself. Words spilled out of my mouth before I took the time to think them through.

"Do you have plans, you know, back at school, for the rest of the weekend?" I asked, unsure of what he would say or if I truly wanted to hear his response. Maybe there would be parties. Maybe there would be wild nights at the bars in town.

Maybe there would be other girls.

He shook his head. "No. Not really. Nothing I couldn't be talked out of." The corner of his mouth puckered into a dimple. "Why?"

I avoided making eye contact with Charlie as I continued to blather on. "It's just that we have a ton of turkey and stuffing and green bean casserole at home and if you didn't have anything else going on at school, I thought you might be interested in coming to our house for the rest of the weekend." I paused to catch my breath. "But you totally don't have to if you don't want to," I added.

I followed Nate's gaze to Brooke, who had wiggled her way inside the liner of Charlie's coat while he was still wearing it. She shivered against him as the last slivers of pale November sun disappeared below the horizon. I got the sense that he was looking to her for approval.

"Mom won't care," Charlie said at last. "There's plenty of space. He's welcome to crash in my room."

I turned to face him and he reached out to take my hand.

"Yeah. Sure. I'd love to come." He held up his duffle. "But I only have one change of clothes and no toothbrush, so maybe we could stop to pick one up somewhere along the way?"

Chapter Sixteen

Fall Semester-First Year

After a microwaved dinner of Thanksgiving leftovers and a recap of the game for my mom, Charlie and Brooke said their goodbyes and headed to their house for the night. I led Nate up the stairs to Charlie's old room, carrying a small bag of toiletries from the corner drugstore as he followed behind, lugging his heavy duffle. I switched on the overhead light as we entered the room.

"This place is amazing," he said, as he set down his things to properly assess the expanse of Charlie's bedroom. "You didn't tell me you live in a mansion."

I felt heat rising to my cheeks. "It's not a mansion, really."

He plopped down heavily onto Charlie's king bed and sprung himself up and down on the mattress several times, testing its durability. "This room is about the size of the first floor of my entire house. And ten of us lived there. I can't imagine what it would have been like having this much room to spread out." He ran his hand over Charlie's thick comforter. "And think about your mom... when you're at school, she has the whole house to herself. Must be kinda lonely."

I reflected upon just how empty our house had always felt and how easy it had been as a child to lose myself in its many nooks and crannies. I remembered escaping from the world for hours at a time, alone with my books, without fear of having to engage in any sort of family routines. How different our childhoods must have been.

I took a tentative step in his direction from where I stopped short in the center of the room, and he immediately pulled me on to the bed beside him. He stretched out so that when he rested on his elbow, he could look directly at me, face to face.

"Tell me what it was like."

"Tell you what *what* was like?"

"What it was like, growing up here?"

There was so little to tell and so much to explain. I didn't know quite where to begin or what he actually wanted to know. I considered the house itself and how all the square footage and interior designers in the world couldn't make a house feel like a home. In truth, I didn't know why my mom hadn't sold it and downsized years ago, but I supposed she had her reasons. Perhaps there were memories she couldn't stand to part from.

"It was okay," I said finally.

"Okay? Are you joking?"

"No. I mean, you're right. The house is amazing. It's beautiful and well-maintained and I never had to worry about not having my own space. I guess I always just kind of had too much space." I glanced around Charlie's room at his old trophies and books and posters of European castles and soccer teams on the walls. "But space without love to fill it up is just space," I said finally.

"But Charlie and Brooke and your mom…"

"Are perfect," I interrupted. "But it's taken so much work to become the family we are now. It hasn't always been this way. For a long time, it was…" I stopped. I didn't know how to describe how life had been before my dad died. It hadn't been horrible. It just wasn't good.

I took a deep breath and tried to explain. "Charlie's so much older than me, you know? By the time I started kindergarten, he was already in middle school. He tried really hard to include me in stuff, but he could only drag his little sister along to so much. I think his way of dealing with the pressure at home was to avoid being here as much as possible. He was involved in every sport and club and spent a lot of time with his friends at their houses. So that meant most of the time, it was just me and mom here in this big, giant house by ourselves. And she did her thing and I did mine. And we both tried to stay out of my father's way when he showed up." I laughed. "I think your family would have probably enjoyed this house a lot more than we did."

"I think we would have destroyed this house," he said, tapping my nose with the tip of his finger. "Can I see the rest?" he asked, hopping off the bed.

"Of course," I replied, following him to the door. "I'll give you the grand tour."

We inspected each floor of the house as if I was a curator of a fine museum. I pointed out what little architecture and history I knew about the three-story Georgian I called home. We crept into attic spaces and peeked into rooms I hadn't explored in years.

"There's not even furniture in here," he commented as we opened the door of a long-forgotten guest room.

"I know. My mom gave up trying to please my dad about decorating the house when I was about ten or eleven. I remember them having this huge fight about some estate auction she wanted to go to. She liked the charm of antique furniture which he considered 'garbage' so Mom told him she was never buying another piece of furniture ever again. And true to her word, she never has. I think there are probably still two or three rooms with nothing in them."

He whistled between his teeth. "My family would have filled them in a heartbeat. With people mostly, not necessarily stuff. But my mom does her best decorating with furnishings off the side of the road."

He grinned at me, waiting for a reaction.

"Stop," I said. "You're not serious."

"Hand to God. The dresser in my bedroom came out of a dumpster. My mom's a 'one man's trash is another man's treasure' kinda woman. And let's just say we have a lot of other people's trash in our house."

"I think I'd like your mom," I told him as I led him out of the room. "She seems practical."

"Insanely practical," he replied, closing the door behind him as we continued down the hall. "I don't know how she raised us all in that tiny house, but she did. I shared a room with two of my brothers, and the day Will left for college was the first night I ever slept in a room by myself. I was fifteen." He ran his fingers along the mahogany wainscoting which ran the length of the hall. "Now that I think about it, it's a wonder we didn't all kill each other off."

"Trust me," I said, "the size of your house doesn't say anything about the quality of the people living inside." I stopped at the door to my bedroom and couldn't decide if it was appropriate to take him inside. I elected to err on the side of prudence and turned on my heel back in the direction of Charlie's room. "Anyway, that's the end of the tour," I called over my shoulder.

I took three steps before I realized he wasn't following me.

"What about your room?" he asked.

"It's right behind you," I replied.

He held out his arms as if to lead the way. "Will you show me?" he asked.

Against my better judgment, I slipped past him and stepped into my bedroom, fumbling with the light switch behind the door. The crystals dangling from the lamp on my nightstand threw glimmers of light off the walls, and I was keenly aware of how feminine and juvenile the room appeared. My Victorian doll house still sat in the far corner, its inhabitants waiting patiently to be brought to life by the imagination of a child who no longer existed. I hadn't thought about the house in ages and was embarrassed by its presence. The piles of stuffed animals and my old unicorn mural spoke of a little girl and not the woman I'd become.

"Purple, huh?" Nate remarked as he gave the room a once over.

"It's actually lavender," I replied, immediately regretting my decision to invite him in. I felt the overwhelming urge to explain why I was still sleeping in a room decorated for an elementary schooler. "My mom and I picked out the color together for my eighth birthday. I was big into purple then, I guess. I don't know why I never thought to repaint it."

He flopped onto the white wicker papasan chair beside my bookshelf and started flipping through my well-worn copy of *To Kill a Mockingbird*. "I don't know," he said. "I don't mind the purple. It brings out the color of your eyes, just like when you wear that purple sweater with the little flowers."

His remark caught me off guard and I replayed it in my head several times before responding. Did he really pay attention to my clothes?

"Okay, smooth talker," I said, aware of just how self-conscious it made me to talk about myself. "What color are my eyes?"

"They're green," he replied without the slightest hesitation.

The tone of his voice disarmed me. He was hurt. Offended by the notion that I didn't believe he thought I was important enough to be memorable. Until that moment I was still under the delusion that our being together was an impossibility. That we were too different to ever really amount to anything other than a college fling. And then it hit me.

He knew the color of my eyes.

He chose leftover turkey with me over the end-of-the-season blow-out with the team.

I took a step closer to where he sat reading the back cover of the book.

"I think I read this in ninth grade. Did you read it for class?"

"No," I replied, taking another step closer. "I read it for fun."

"That sounds about right," he laughed, tossing the book onto the carpet. "It's the one about the girl whose dad's a lawyer, right?"

"Her name is Scout."

"Yeah. I remember. It was a good book."

"I thought so too," I said, as my final step placed me squarely between his knees. I knelt down in front of him, resting my hands on his thighs. I wanted to tell him how I was feeling. I needed to tell him.

"I've been trying to figure out what in the world this is…"

"The book?"

I chewed nervously at a hangnail. "No. Not the book." I started again. I needed him to understand. "I'm trying to figure out what it is that you and I are doing?"

He shrugged his shoulders. "We're having fun."

"That's not true."

"You're not having fun?"

I rolled my eyes. "Yes of course I'm having fun. But that's not all this is."

"It's not?"

"No." I took a deep breath and gathered my courage. I wasn't typically very direct with people because I never like to show my hand. But in a very uncharacteristic move, I was about to lay all my cards on the table. "You like me," I said finally.

He was smiling now, leaning forward in the chair so that I could feel the warmth of his breath on my face. "I do?"

"You do. I didn't realize it at first either because you're so how you are, and I'm so how I am, but you're here, at my house, and you could be anywhere. You're not at those places though. You chose to be here with me."

"Maybe I couldn't stomach the thought of eating in one of the dining halls tonight," he countered. "Or maybe I just didn't want to listen to McNaulty mouthing off about his spectacular defensive maneuvers for the rest of the weekend."

"Liar," I said, picking idly at a pull in the sleeve of my sweater because I was no longer able to look him in the eye. "You're here because you like me."

Without responding to my accusation and before I could protest, he lifted me from the floor and sat me on his lap. The wicker papasan creaked beneath our weight and although I worried briefly about breaking it, I quickly decided I didn't care about the fate of the chair. Nate cradled my face gently in his hands.

"I don't like you, Melody Johnson."

His declaration shook my confidence and made me question my judgment. I bowed my head, humiliated. "You don't?"

"No," he said as he lifted my chin. "I love you. And what's more than that, I think I need you. All semester I've been caring about all this stuff I've never cared about before. I'm doing extra homework. I'm finishing assignments on time. I'm eating healthier. I'm washing laundry. I've been trying to figure out what the heck is going on with me. And then today, when I made that touchdown, the first thing that came into my head was 'I hope Melody saw.' It's like I didn't really care about what anyone else thought. Suddenly, you're the only one I want to impress. And when I saw you in the stands, it all made sense."

I was confused. He didn't like me because he *loved* me?

"What made sense?" I whispered.

"The way I've been feeling. These last few months I've been so busy trying to fill your life with fun that I didn't realize what you've been doing to me."

"What have I been doing?"

"You've been giving me a reason to be a better person. A better student. A better player. A better friend. I want you to keep me around because I like being around you, Mel. I want you to like me as much as I like you." He kissed me gently on the lips. "I want you to love me as much as I love you."

His words seemed ridiculous coming out of his mouth. He wasn't being the big, dumb jock I had him pegged for on that very first day. The one I assumed was incapable of feeling anything other than pride and self-ambition. He was absolutely nothing like the person I kept expecting him to be.

He was better. So much better.

What I wanted to do in that moment was melt into a puddle on the floor. What I did instead was punch him in the shoulder as hard as I could. "That's for giving me a heart attack," I said just before he silenced me with his lips once again.

The next hour of my life involved a lot of touching, kissing, and the removal of clothing. I had never felt so cherished or so completely sure of anything in my entire life. We talked in hushed whispers like conspirators in a crime about what loving each other would look like now that we'd both confessed how we felt. And then my mom, who I hoped had forgotten we existed, poked her head in to announce she was going to bed and that we should do the same.

Separately.

In our own rooms.

The night Nate stayed at my house for the first time was the night I fell hopelessly and shamelessly in love with him. Before that night, I was on the brink. I liked him. A lot. And he'd become a welcome fixture in my day to day life. But the night he spent under the roof of my childhood home was the night I accepted there was no turning back. I handed over my heart to Nate Johansen.

The weekend flew by in a whirlwind of introductions and family gatherings. On Saturday we met Brooke's parents at our favorite outdoor ice rink, and it wasn't until I saw Nate struggling with his laces that I realized he'd never been ice skating before.

"At least the season's already over if I break my leg," he joked as I helped him onto the ice.

After pulling me down with him half a dozen times, he finally started to get the hang of it and before long was racing Charlie around the rink. The two of them hit it off immediately and Brooke and I sat together at dinner lamenting our abandonment.

"He's adorable," she said. "If someone that size can still qualify as being adorable."

"I think he can," I agreed. "Only don't tell him I said that."

"It's too bad he and Charlie don't seem to have anything in common," she joked as we watched the men, heads together, embroiled in a serious conversation about which sports were the most difficult to play based on endurance versus skill. They'd been debating it for half an hour and had barely come up for air when their burgers arrived.

When dinner was over they interrogated us in the parking lot, coming at us like two members of the CIA.

"Charlie said we can go to his house tomorrow to watch the Redskins. It's the one o'clock game. Do we have time to go or do you want to head back to school early?" He cocked his head to the side and grinned.

How could I say no?

"Yes, we can stay for the game," I relented willingly, "but then you'll have to drive us back so I can study in the car."

"It's a deal," he replied, throwing his arm around my shoulder as we approached the car.

"I would say I've never seen anything more hilarious," Brooke said to Charlie, taking him under the arm, "but he reminds me a lot of you at that age. You practically camped out at my house, remember?"

"I do remember," Charlie smiled. Then he turned to me. "Thanks for letting him come."

Chapter Seventeen

Summer Break – Second to Third Year

Vicki started crying about twenty minutes north of the police station. There was no warning whimper, just silence and then screaming. I ventured a glance into the rearview mirror and could see her reflection in the baby mirror I'd ingeniously rigged to the headrest above her. She looked like a possessed raisin, all scrunched and crimson. She was awake and she was hungry.

"It's gonna be okay, bug-a-boo. We're almost there and then I'll feed you. I promise. I'm so sorry about the long drive, but sometimes we have to do stuff we don't want to do. That's just the way it goes."

She continued to wail, ignoring my uncensored reflections on life. I didn't feel the need to sugar coat it for her. That's the sort of aunt I was going to be.

As we pulled into the parking lot of the county police headquarters, my head was throbbing. After slipping into the closest space I could find, I grabbed a bottle from the diaper bag, grateful I had the forethought to prepare one before we left. Because she wasn't able to hold the bottle for herself, I slid into the back seat of the car to feed her, slipping the nipple of the bottle between her eager lips to make amends and silence her hysteria.

Once pacified, I turned my attention to the precinct and the daunting task before me. After disconnecting Vicki's seat from its base and hoisting it out of the car, we approached the run-down building, maintained by tax dollars which had long since been appropriated to other causes. Paint peeled from the windowsills and I nearly tripped on a large crack in the sidewalk. As I struggled with Vicki through the heavy double doors and security clearance, I caught a glimpse of my reflection in the glass and realized how pathetic I must have appeared to the officers; an unwed teen mom come to rescue her stoner baby-daddy from jail. Poor thing. Another statistic. I felt like a character from a late-night reality TV show.

Vicki, for her part, began attracting unsolicited attention as we approached the front desk. The dainty looking receptionist, who was surely someone's maw-maw, craned her neck around the corner of the counter to get a better view.

"Well my goodness, isn't she just the sweetest thing? How old is she?"

My response rushed out, all in one breath, in an attempt to legitimize my situation. "She's a little over three months but she was born premature, so she's small. But she's not mine. I mean, I didn't steal her or anything because she's my brother's baby." I sounded like a maniac and I knew it. "She's my niece," I said at last.

Perhaps she thought I was lying to cover something up because all at once Vicki's allure faded and the maw-maw 'mmm-hmmed' condescendingly through her pursed lips.

"I see. And what can we do here for you today?"

My hasty departure and concern for Vicki initially overshadowed the potential humiliation associated with bailing Nate out of jail, but faced with the reality of the woman's bitter disapproval, I was forced to acknowledge my own embarrassment. I was petrified she would think I was a bad person, and for a second, I considered walking away. In the end, however, my loyalty to Nate would not allow me to leave. He needed me and I loved him. There was nothing more to it than that.

"I'm here about Nate Johansen," I began, wording my reason carefully so as not to implicate myself. "I received a phone call earlier today about coming to pick him up."

"Mmm hmm," Maw-maw said again, scanning her computer screen. "Oh yes, here he is." She clicked her tongue, alerting me to just how offended she was by Nate's transgressions. "I see he's being detained just down the hall. Got picked up for buying drugs right outside the station last night. Not too bright, that one. I can call for someone to take you back to fill out the necessary paperwork." She nodded to a row of chairs against the wall. "You can take a seat over there while you wait."

I dragged both Vicki and the diaper bag over to the waiting area where I finally unlatched her harness, releasing her from her constraints. I cuddled her against my cheek and whispered heartfelt apologies for our dismal state. Satisfied with her meal and happy to be out of the seat, she rewarded me with another of her goofy smiles. She was my ray of light in an otherwise gloomy afternoon.

Not long after the paperwork was complete and his bail was paid, a remorseful Nate appeared in the hallway just beyond a locked gate. The same weather-beaten officer who executed the bail led him in my direction. He wouldn't look me in the eyes. His shame was far too great.

Released to his own recognizance, he held the exit door for me as the heat of the late afternoon sun overpowered us.

"It's hot today," he commented nonchalantly as we shuffled along the weed-infested gravel lot.

"I hadn't noticed," I replied curtly. "I've been too busy taking care of other people's problems."

He recoiled, stung by the venom of my response. My initial reaction was to apologize but before I spoke, I quickly reminded myself there was no reason to be sorry. Nate was well past due for taking responsibility for his own behavior, and I wished for the millionth time that Sam had never died.

Vicki didn't put up a fight as I restrapped her into the car seat and without any further incidents, we were off.

"Where am I taking you?" I asked, attempting to keep the irritation out of my voice as we reached the stop sign at the edge of the parking lot. A mirage shimmered on the boiling surface of the asphalt and I stared at it, unable to look at Nate. "I need to know which way to turn."

I waited, listening to the steady whoosh of the air conditioning blowing cool air at my cheek. Nate sighed, his shoulders rising and falling with great effort.

"I'm sorry, Mel," he said finally.

I bowed my head. I didn't want him to be sorry. I wanted him to admit he'd hit bottom and do something about it. My voice broke as I continued to avoid the very large elephant in the room.

"Sorry doesn't tell me which way to go. Am I taking you home? Do you want to go to your sister's?"

He remained silent and although I didn't want to face him, I knew I couldn't avoid him any longer. His chin was buried in his chest but he must have felt me staring because he finally replied.

"I was kind of hoping that maybe I could go to your house," he said.

Coming home with me was the last request I expected. We hadn't seen each other all summer. Not a single visit or invitation south. Even worse, he'd only called three times. Four if I included his appeal to bail him out of jail. He texted me twice a week to check in – a quick 'how are you' or 'I miss you' but nothing of any substance.

I was losing him. Or perhaps I'd already lost him and was just holding on to the idea of who he used to be. Of how we used to be together. In that moment I knew unless he found a way to break the chains of his addiction I would never be able to take Nate home again. I reached out to him, laying my hand on his knee and was overcome by the depth of emotion the simple touch invoked.

I looked past him, over his shoulder at another mirage. "I don't know if that's the best idea. Things haven't exactly been great with us, you know?"

He coughed weakly and adjusted his position in the car's tiny seat so he could face me. His eyes were bloodshot - whether from crying or lack of sleep or pills, I didn't know, but I suppressed the urge to be sympathetic.

"I know," he said finally. "It's just that, you came. I didn't know if you would, but you did. And then, while I've been waiting for you, I've been thinking that maybe things would be better if we just spent some more time together. You know, like before."

The mirage disappeared and reappeared as cars drove across it. It was there, and then it wasn't. Just like Nate. I wasn't ready to let him go but he was already gone. It was almost as if he had never really existed at all. As I stared past him, I wondered how long it would take to convince myself that our relationship had never happened so that maybe I could go back to school and move on with my life.

"How long has it been?"

He shrugged lazily. "Since what?"

"Since you used, Nate? How long will it be before you feel the need to stone yourself into oblivion again?"

He turned on me in an instant, shifting from acquiescing to furious without missing a beat. "Shut up, Melody," he spat with contempt. With a simple, albeit antagonistic question, I'd evoked the drug-addled beast inside him. But for the first time, I didn't care.

Because I was angry too.

"This isn't okay anymore," I growled, keeping my voice low so I didn't upset Vicki. "You can't continue to treat me this way. It's not fair. And even though it's my own fault I keep convincing myself to just hold on a little longer, hoping eventually you'll go back to the way you used to be, I'm done being strung along. You are not the same person I fell in love with, Nate, and you've done a good job over the past few months of convincing me that you will never be that person again, no matter how long I wait or how badly I want it to come true. So, I'm done. This is the last time I enable you."

The air felt as muggy on the inside of the car as it was on the outside, but as I pressed the button to crank up the air conditioning, my temperature continued to rise. Blood pulsed through my ears as I waited for him to respond. I wanted him to say something, *anything*, to acknowledge the destruction he had caused. I wanted him to feel the depth of my anguish. Instead, he rubbed the callouses on the palm of his hand, as if they were unseen pressure points with the power to alleviate his pain.

"Is that really how you feel?" he said at last.

Vicki whimpered in the back seat, and I knew if I started driving she would fall right to sleep. I needed to get moving before she worked herself into a frenzy or I'd be adding "screaming baby" to my growing list of problems. It was time to make a decision, but that was easier said than done.

The truth was, although I didn't want to say goodbye, it was time for me to move on with my life. The constant stress of maintaining a relationship with an addict was exhausting, like caring for a festering wound without even the most basic understanding of first aid. I knew I needed to properly bandage the emotional lacerations created by his addiction so I could begin to heal. I was finally ready to accept that while he was still in my life, hope would continue to pick at the scabs and I would continue to bleed. I was done wondering when it was all going to end. It was time to stop pretending we were ever going to be okay.

Before I could stop myself, the words spilled out.

"I don't have the strength to worry over you any longer. I hate sitting up all hours of the night wondering if you're okay. I hate wondering if today will be the day you take too many pills and don't wake up. Sam's death, the pills, your refusal to move on... they've made you a shell of who you used to be and it breaks my heart every single day. I nag you. You ignore me. You've turned me into a person I don't like and you and I both know this isn't what I signed up for. This isn't who we are supposed to be together. I love you, Nate, but I don't see any future for us if this is all there is left. And I know this isn't your fault. I know you're sick and your addiction and the way you act are only symptoms of that illness, but I can't make you better. Only you can do that."

I tried not to cry as I waited for him to react. I searched his face for signs that he was angry or defensive or devastated.

But he didn't appear to be any of those things. Instead, without a word, he reached out to press his thumb gently across my bottom lip, his eyes closed as if in prayer, and then, without a word, he crawled out of the car, shutting the door carefully behind him.

I sat in stunned silence, watching him in the rearview mirror as he crossed the parking lot back toward the police station. Vicki's cries of protest intensified and I remained perched on the threshold between going after him and driving away. My grip tightened on the steering wheel as she began to scream in earnest. It was time to make a decision and I didn't know if it was because of our shared history or in spite of it, but in that instant I knew the decision had already been made.

Chapter Eighteen

Summer Break – Second to Third Year

From upstairs in my bedroom I heard the familiar sound of the doorbell's gong. I wasn't expecting anyone and decided without looking out the window that it was probably just a delivery my mom could bring in when she got home from work. And then the doorbell rang a second time. And a third.

I took the stairs two at a time since it was clear from the steady rhythm of knocks and rings that whoever graced my doorstop was growing impatient.

"Nate!" I cried, leaping into his arms when I opened the door.

"I thought I was gonna have to sleep out here!" he laughed, crushing me in his embrace.

"You weren't supposed to be here until tomorrow," I murmured into his chest as I breathed in his sweet, musky scent.

He released me and backed onto the porch. "My shift at work got cancelled for tonight so I thought I'd surprise you. But I can go back home if you want," he teased.

"NO!" I replied, pulling him into the foyer. "Are those for me?" I asked, noticing the bouquet of daisies clutched in his fist.

"My lady," he bowed, extending the flowers toward me.

"How very chivalrous," I said as I accepted the daisies and thanked him with a proper kiss. A mixture of excitement and relief washed over me and the memory of his touch returned - the way his bottom lip fit perfectly beneath my own as if it had been formed just for that space. There was the gentle warmth I'd grown accustomed to, but also an urgency that was new. It had been three weeks since summer break began and the daily phone calls, although appreciated, were barely cutting it. Nothing beat the gift of having the person you love physically present in your life. Apparently, Nate felt the same way.

"Are we alone?" he asked, craning his neck to see into the kitchen.

I knew what he was thinking. It was nice to know some things never changed.

"Yes, but only for another fifteen minutes or so. Mom should be home from work soon."

"Fifteen minutes is plenty of time," he grinned.

I elbowed him in the gut. "I'm sure we'll get some time to ourselves at the beach. But for now, the last thing you need is to get on my mom's bad side. I told her you were a gentleman."

"Why'd you lie to her like that?" he asked, tossing his duffle beside the door.

I took his hand and led him into the kitchen, ignoring his advances. "Come on. Let's find something to put these flowers in and maybe you can live up to her expectations by helping me start dinner."

Mom was as surprised as I was to see Nate had arrived a day early but was thrilled to have the extra help loading the food and gear into the car the next day. Growing up, our family's yearly trip to the beach had always been the highlight of my summer. After my dad died, we stopped going for several years, but when Brooke and Charlie got married we resumed the tradition, adding Brooke and her parents to the mix. And after spending time with him over spring break, I was delighted when Charlie suggested it would be fun to invite Nate along as well. I was even more excited when Nate happily accepted the invitation, and although he swore my family couldn't be half as crazy as his own, I secretly worried spending a week with all of us might spell the end of our relationship.

My theory was tested the very first day.

While I had visions of relaxing beside Nate on the beach and maybe even dipping my toes in the surf, Brooke's father had other plans. Unbeknownst to the rest of us, he'd reserved a chartered, eight-hour fishing excursion, chumming for bluefish just off the coast. So instead of the lazy morning I had planned, we were all corralled into the back of Brooke's parents' van before sunrise so we could be to the boat by 7 AM. I couldn't have been more disappointed.

"This is not my idea of a good time," I whispered to Nate as I rubbed sleep out of my eyes.

"Are you kidding?" he countered, staring out the car window as the reflection of the rising sun rippled across the waves. "This is gonna be awesome! I've never been ocean fishing before."

With so many children, his family wasn't able to afford vacations while he was growing up. As I watched him, glued to the seaside scenery on our way to the dock, it occurred to me that I'd begun taking our yearly vacation for granted.

"It's disgusting," I told him. "Do you have any idea what chum smells like?"

"Chopped up dead fish? I can imagine," he replied, crinkling his nose. "But think of how much fun it's gonna be to reel in those fighting blues!"

It was endearing to experience the wonder of the day through Nate's eyes. He took to the chumming process like he was born to shove fish carcasses into a grinder. At least if he was enjoying it, I didn't have to.

"Check out how the blood creates a film on the water," he called to me above the boat's engine. "I wonder if it'll bring in any sharks?"

Sadly for Nate, it didn't bring any sharks, but it did end up bringing in dozens of bluefish. He listened attentively to the boat captain who explained how to rig our lines with various weights and sinkers. I helped bait his hook with a piece of smelt, and when we finally released our lines into the water, he was the first to snag a fish.

"It's pulling hard," he laughed. "I wonder how big he is?"

I handed my own line off to Charlie and watched Nate reel in his catch. He had the same look of determination and breathless anticipation he displayed on the football field, and I could not have been more proud as I watched him wrestle the fish into the boat.

"He's gigantic!" Charlie exclaimed, patting Nate on the back as the ten-pound bluefish tossed itself around the hull of the boat. "Now the hard part is getting that hook out of its mouth. Those things will bite your finger off!"

The three men worked carefully to free the fish from the line and tossed it into the live box without incurring any injuries. Meanwhile Brooke caught her first fish while our mothers sat chatting in the bow of the boat. Any other year I would have joined them with my sun hat and a book, but I couldn't tear myself away from Nate's excitement over every catch.

"I've got another one on!" he cried, reeling his line eagerly while he fought to keep his balance. "I don't think it's as big as the first one, but it's still fighting mad."

Our family ended up catching eighteen fish, which Nate reveled in cleaning with Charlie when we returned to shore. He joined me in the kitchen, sunburned and salt-kissed as I battered the fresh fillets in cracker crumbs for dinner.

"That was the best day ever," he sighed, leaning down to wrap his arms around my neck from behind.

"Stinky fish really do it for ya, huh?"

"Among other things," he said, nibbling on my ear.

I could feel the heat of his skin pressing against my bare shoulders and knew my fears about him being overwhelmed by my family were unfounded. He fit right in to our particular brand of crazy, probably even better than I did myself.

"How about shucking corn? I'd totally love if you were into shucking corn."

"What's my reward if I am?"

I set the fillet onto the baking sheet and turned to face him, standing on my tip toes to kiss the fullness of his lips.

"There's more where that came from," I told him, "and if you're an especially good shucker, I'll let you walk me to the ice cream place down the street for dessert."

He feigned the giddiness of a preteen girl. "Making out and ice cream?" he squealed.

"I know. I'm sort of a dream come true. Now get on with your shucking."

Dinner was delicious, as was the ice cream.

The making out was pretty amazing too.

By the end of the week, my family was completely smitten with Nate. After happily participating in every one of our adventures, even posing for one of those ridiculous old-timey photos, he earned an honorary spot in the Wallace/Johnson clan. He and Charlie battled it out on the prehistoric themed mini-golf course, with Charlie winning by a stroke when he sank a hole-in-one through the legs of the flaming tyrannosaurus. He squeezed into a go-cart car he was entirely too big for and served as official bag carrier during our trip to the outlets. And on the last night of our vacation, he held my hand as we strolled along breaking surf.

"Your family's a lot of fun," he told me.

"We are," I agreed. "Although I have to admit that I sort of missed having my dad around this week. He wasn't perfect. He was actually really difficult, mostly. But on vacation, here at the beach, it was almost as if he turned into someone else. He became the most fun version of himself. I'm always reminded of that Dad when we're here." I swung Nate's hand by my side. "I'd like to think he would have enjoyed having you along with us."

He maneuvered to avoid a breaking wave. "You think he would have liked me?"

I laughed, considering the short list of things my father actually liked. "I think he would have put on his perma-smile and pretended to even if he didn't. But yeah, deep down, I think he would have been a fool not to."

The surf washed in a foamy line of shells and seaweed. He stopped to pick up a shell that came to rest at his feet. It was a perfectly formed moon shell. He handed it to me.

"Brooke told me the same thing about Branson - that he would have liked me. Said they played football together in the yard all the time when they were kids and that he would have loved having a real football player in the family." He stopped to pick up another shell and threw it into the waves. "You've had a lot of death in your family. Life's pretty fragile, isn't it?"

I looked up at him, illuminated by the moon reflecting off the ocean. It was strange to hear him being philosophical.

"Death is a part of life," I said. "It is what it is."

"Death should come at the end of life," he countered. "Not in the beginning or the middle. It's the order of things."

"Until it isn't," I said pragmatically.

He fingered a length of hair that had blown free from my ponytail in the warm ocean breeze and tucked it behind my ear.

"I love you, Mel," he said. "I would have never guessed when we met just how strong you are. You're a lot tougher than you look."

My heart swelled knowing he thought I was resilient. I'd never really thought of myself that way, but I supposed it was true. It felt good to hear the compliment coming from him. And then I considered how different he was from how I'd imagined him to be when we first met. I remembered assuming he was emotionally lacking, but the truth was exactly the opposite. His heart was as big as his brawny exterior and he never missed an opportunity to be kind.

"I love you too," I told him, placing my head on his chest. "But not because you're tough. I love you because you're not nearly as tough as you look."

Chapter Nineteen

Summer Break – Second to Third Year

What remained of summer seemed to drag on endlessly. To fill the hours outside my babysitting responsibilities, my mom encouraged me to focus on doing things that would bring me joy. My first inclination was to go to a concert with some friends from high school, but I was disappointed to discover we no longer shared the same interests, ambitions, or taste in music. I came away feeling as though we were no longer companions but just a random group of people I used to know.

Disillusioned but undeterred, I racked my brain for other possible activities, eventually remembering a conversation with Senator Turner about an event she was hosting at the country club. After initially declining her invitation, I ended up attending the fundraiser I privately dubbed 'November's Coming Campaign Gala (No Special Interest Groups Allowed).' Although it was exactly as boring as I expected it to be, I impressed myself with my ability to make small talk and even managed to establish a few new connections.

At his request, and because it had always been my favorite summer tradition, I snuck in a morning of kayaking and a picnic lunch with Charlie on one of his rare days off. When we finished eating, Brooke arrived with Vicki, and after slathering her with copious amounts of baby zinc oxide, we dipped her toes into the water, much to her delight. She didn't even seem to mind our ineptitude when her diaper absorbed half the lake and ended up weighing more than she did.

When I could think of nothing left to do, I indulged my mom in a shopping expedition for pots and pans and a coffee maker to outfit the apartment I'd be sharing with Lesley and Kara when classes resumed. She'd pestered me for weeks about needing to prepare, but like everything else I was trying to avoid, I let it go until the last minute. As we perused nonstick and stainless steel, she commented that having my own place signaled the final leg of my transition into adulthood. I didn't know why but the thought of it made me sad. Perhaps it was because my future seemed so vague and undetermined.

While I crammed a lot of diversions into the final weeks of my vacation, I didn't do the one thing I was actually trying to do.

Despite my best efforts, I wasn't able to forget about Nate.

As much as I tried not to, I thought about him constantly. The more I tried to think about other things, the more he squeezed his way into my psyche. Every song I heard reminded me of him; if not the words themselves than the memory of us hearing the song together. I couldn't eat without being reminded of our time together - when we stopped at an all-night diner for waffles after a concert at 3 AM, or how much I loved his famous grilled Swiss cheese and tomato sandwiches, or the time he snarfed soda so badly through his nose that he couldn't swallow properly for a week.

The hardest part was watching Brooke and Charlie together, the way his hand would brush against her hip as they passed by one another – a touch that spoke volumes without a word being spoken. I envied their secret language of facial expressions and subtle mannerisms. It reminded me of how it might have been for Nate and me, if only...

I began packing for school no less than ten times but every attempt left me bleary eyed, surrounded by memories of all the days we'd spent together. I realized, as I packed away a photo of the two of us sharing a sundae, that I'd only spent five days at school without him - the five days before we met. Now I'd be facing all of them without him. No being walked to class. No surprise visits in the middle of the afternoon. No security of someone always having my back.

It was of little comfort knowing that my decision to break up with him had no bearing on his absence from school. His grades were so low he'd been academically dismissed from not only the football team but from classes as well, so regardless of how we ended, he wasn't coming back. Not this year. Probably not ever.

With less than twelve hours before it was time to leave, I buckled down and forced myself to focus on doing what needed to be done. I knew I would be fine. I had wonderful friends and a solid career path. And as everyone was quick to remind me, there were plenty of other fish in the sea.

As I packed up the last of my shorts and t-shirts, I heard a gentle knock on my bedroom door.

"Come in," I called absently.

My mom opened the door, only a crack at first, and peered into my room, which was still purple and full of entirely too many stuffed animals.

"Need any help?" she asked.

I contemplated whether I needed to take all three of my jeans shorts and returned my oldest pair to my closet.

"No," I replied, "I don't need any help, but I wouldn't mind the company."

Mom didn't throw the door open but instead slid carefully into my room as if she was entering a sacred space. She lingered just beyond the doorway and rocked nervously on her heels while I continued to make important wardrobe decisions.

"Are you excited? About school starting, I mean?" she asked as she skimmed her finger across the accumulated dust on my dresser.

"I guess," I replied without giving her question much thought.

She took another step into the room and began rearranging knickknacks – a picture frame here, a flower vase there.

"Are you looking forward to any of your new classes?"

I tried to remember what I was taking. "Honestly, Mom, I don't even know what I signed up for any more. It feels like a lifetime since enrollment so I guess it'll be a surprise when I get there." I folded my favorite 'Save the Tree Frogs' shirt and laid it in my bag.

"Oh," she said, clearly upset that she hadn't hit upon a topic I was willing to discuss. "Do you have any big plans with Lesley and the others?"

"Not that I know of. I haven't really thought about it." I closed my underwear drawer and watched her, still milling about the periphery of my room. Although she pretended to peruse my bookshelf, I knew she had no interest in my choice of literature, and the reason for her visit was suddenly clear.

She was worried about me.

"Are you here because of Nate?" I asked.

She returned a book to the shelf and spun to face me, a small smile playing on her lips.

"Is it that obvious?"

I hoisted my bag off the bed and chucked it on the floor to make room for us both to sit down. I motioned for her to join me.

"We broke up, Mom. A few weeks ago."

I watched her face carefully for signs of relief or perhaps even joy. Instead, she leaned in to gather me into her arms.

"I'm so sorry, Melody," she said. "I know how much you cared for him."

Until the moment she touched me I hadn't realized how desperately in need of human contact I actually was. I yielded to her, folding myself into her embrace, and before I knew they were coming, tears began streaming down my face. She smoothed my hair, as she'd done when I was a child, and whispered words of consolation.

"It's going to be okay," she said.

"I know I'm going to be okay, but Mom, I feel like I abandoned him. It's been awful. I keep going back and forth between being relieved that it's over and being miserable because I've let him down. He was counting on me."

She lifted my chin to brush a tear off my cheek. "What about you counting on him? The street goes both ways you know."

"I know. And that's why I ended it. But I can't help being sad about what might have been."

"It's a loss that needs to be mourned," she said wisely.

I wiped my eyes with the bottom of my t-shirt. "It feels obnoxious to cry when I was the one who ended things."

"No, honey, you didn't end things. Things ended when Nate made a choice to take the easy way out."

The last rays of evening sun cast long shadows across my floor and caused dust to sparkle in the air. When I was a child I'd believed the dust was magic. Now I knew that dust was just dust.

Like pain was just pain.

"That's just the thing. I don't think he chose to feel the way he felt or react the way he did. It was never a conscious decision. In his own head he feels obligated to ruin his life, and I'm convinced that even though it doesn't make sense to us, it makes perfect sense to him. I just wish there was a way that I could make it better. If only Sam had never gotten benched."

"What's done is done," she said.

"What's done is done," I repeated.

She kissed me gently on the head and left me to finish my packing. As I gathered my makeup and toiletries from the bathroom, I kept thinking about how unfair it all was; Sam's hurt wrist, Nate's poor performance with Sam and stellar performance with Barnes, and the coach's decision to sit Sam out. If only Sam hadn't blamed Nate outright, perhaps Nate wouldn't have felt so responsible for his death.

It wasn't the first time the thought had crossed my mind, but it was the first time I allowed myself to speculate about how I might be able to change Nate's fate. Perhaps what was done wasn't actually done after all.

****

On the night of my eighteenth birthday, Brooke and Charlie gave me a special gift - a watch with the face of a lion on it. While I thought the timepiece was beautiful, its significance was initially lost on me, and it wasn't until later in the evening, as I headed out the door to meet my friends for dinner, that Charlie approached me with his heartfelt request.

"I wanted to talk to you about the watch…"

"It's really nice, Charlie. I love it," I told him, glancing at my wrist to confirm not only that I was wearing it but also that I was late.

"Brooke picked it out. The lion has special meaning for her."

"I'll be sure to say something to her," I replied as I shrugged my jacket over my shoulders.

In one swift motion he glided across the foyer and positioned himself in front of the door. He obviously didn't want me to leave.

"What is it?" I asked, defeated.

"It will only take two minutes, but I promised her I'd say something to you today and I can't lie to her when she asks. Cuz you know her, she's gonna ask."

I sat on the bottom step of the foyer staircase, resigned to the fact that I would be the last to arrive to my own birthday dinner. Everyone knew, once my brother had you in his crosshairs, avoiding him was not an option. He sat beside me, mollified and began his monologue.

"You know how she and I feel about time travel, with all the problems we both had. I don't think we ever told you, but during her second trip the changes she made led to Mrs. Cooper's death as well as her parents' divorce. Not to mention that she broke up with me. She really ruined things trying to save Branson. And of course, we all know how I would have ended up if Victoria hadn't used her own trip to keep me out of jail. What I'm saying is, now that you're old enough to take your trip, remember how dangerous it can be. I can't forbid you from using it, and I certainly can't prevent it, but I can keep reminding you that it's not worth risking everything you have for a chance to go back. The watch is that reminder. When you look at it, remember time only goes forward. The present and the future are all you have. No good can come from venturing to the past." He hesitated briefly, and I could tell he was going over his speech in his head to be sure he hadn't left out any important details.

He was nothing if not thorough.

"Oh yeah, and the lion…"

I glanced down at its golden mane.

"What about the lion?"

"It's from Brooke. Apparently, on her trips, she took a little clay lion she made for Branson when they were kids. It was kind of a talisman or good luck charm or something, but anyway, she sees the lion as a source of strength and bravery. And that was her gift to you. Be brave in your decisions. Let the lion be a source of strength for you like it was for her."

I continued gazing at the watch, focusing solely on the time. If I hit every traffic light green I would only be ten minutes late.

"Is that all you needed to tell me?" I asked.

He ran his fingers through his hair, tousling it beyond its already disheveled state.

"Yeah. I guess that's it. Sorry to keep you from your friends."

I popped up off the step and hurried to the door.

"No big deal," I called over my shoulder as I turned the handle, "and thanks for the watch. I like it a lot. Tell Brooke thanks too."

****

After our initial conversation, Charlie only mentioned the watch and its symbolism a handful of times, and I, for my part, always blew him off. Brooke and Charlie were notoriously overprotective, and when it came to their dislike of time travel, they could be complete zealots. They both used their trips and they both made mistakes, but Brooke was purposefully trying to change the past and since Charlie had no idea his parents' deaths were linked – it was no wonder things didn't work out for them.

I wouldn't make the same mistakes.

I fished through my jewelry box and quickly located the watch in the drawer with my other bracelets and trinkets. The lion's golden face shone up at me and I ran my finger across the beveled crystal.

"Hello, Lion," I whispered.

Brooke intended for the lion to serve as a reminder of strength and bravery, but I felt much more like a coward as I looked into its eyes. Since the moment I left him in the police station parking lot, I couldn't shake the feeling that I'd abandoned Nate. I thought, quite naively, I could walk away from the relationship without looking back, but as I cradled the watch in my hands there was no way I could go on pretending I was still the person I was before.

With Nate I discovered that love was messy, like the piles of clay I played with as a child. We showed up to the relationship as individually colored globs, and in the beginning, it was still possible to make out our distinct colors, where one shade stopped and the other began. He was orange. I was green. But over time, as our relationship grew, the clay got smooshed and shaped, causing our colors to swirl together so thoroughly that it was impossible to pull them back apart. It took breaking up with him to realize I couldn't cut that new glob in half and shove the two pieces back into their original containers. There was no more green. There was no more orange.

We were just two messy globs of brown.

Nate's love changed me, for whatever it was worth, and I knew for a fact I had changed him too. I kept thinking about the year I spent wandering in the darkness after my dad died, and I considered how fortunate I was that Charlie saw fit to pull me out of the cave I was in. If he had never returned to save me, would I have graduated? Lost my friends? Been out on the street?

I shuddered to think.

Now I worried, if I continued to absolve myself from any responsibility, would there be anyone left to save Nate from his dark place? He was out there, alone and afraid, a messy glob of brown just like me, and there was no way I could live with myself if I didn't make one last attempt to bring the old Nate back.

"I'm gonna need some of that courage," I whispered to the lion, "cuz it looks to me like there's only one option left."

Chapter Twenty

Fall Semester – Third Year

Lesley jabbed me on the back of my arm. "Mel, you're totally distracted. What the heck?"

"Huh?" I mumbled, looking up from the notebook on my lap.

"Groceries! I was asking about groceries for the tenth time. I'm going to the store after class. Do you need anything?"

I quickly mulled over a mental inventory of my stash in the fridge. "Nah. I think I'm good. Thanks for asking though."

She threw her backpack over her shoulders, stepping out of the galley kitchen into the den where I was sprawled out on the sofa. "What in the world has you so preoccupied these days? And don't tell me school because we've barely even started."

"It's nothing important," I said, closing the notebook with a loud slap.

"You're a bad liar, Melody Johnson, but it's fine. Have your secrets." She winked at me. "I'll be back before dinner," she called over her shoulder as the door closed behind her.

I was relieved to finally have the apartment to myself because she was right - I wasn't working on homework, although I'd already finished the handful of projects my professors assigned the week before. Instead, I was making a detailed list of the events leading up to Sam and Nate's fight. I'd already spoken with most of their friends, including each of the players who witnessed their confrontation in the locker room on the day of the accident. There was only one other person I still needed to hunt down.

As soon as Lesley's car was safely out of the parking lot, I grabbed my bike and headed across Grounds. It was going to take a little luck with the traffic lights and some fast pedaling if I was going to make it to the gym before football practice was over so I could ambush the coach before he left. It was time to grill him for information.

"Who did you say you were again?" he asked as he hurried across the pavement.

I raced behind him, towing my bike along beside me. "I'm Melody Johnson, Nate Johansen's girlfriend. Or ex-girlfriend I guess."

He turned sharply on his heel, stopping in the middle of the road. "I banked on that kid, you know that?" He was angry now, irritated to irate in just under a second. "When I recruited him, I expected he would play all four years."

I wanted to tell him that he didn't hold the monopoly on people Nate let down, but I thought better of it as I psyched myself up to deliver the speech I'd prepared.

"I know he disappointed a lot of people with his behavior over the past year, but I'm trying now to get to the root of his problems. I just wondered if you wouldn't mind telling me exactly what happened during practice in the days before Sam's death."

"Stupid kid," he mumbled under his breath as he fumbled for his keys and continued walking toward his truck. I didn't know to which kid he was referring – Sam or Nate or me.

"Please, Coach, I just need a minute of your time."

He stopped again, this time sighing heavily as he rested the palm of his hand on the hood of someone's decade-old commuter.

"You think I don't blame myself for what happened?" he asked rhetorically without turning to face me. "You think I don't wonder what would have happened if I had just let him play with that injury? Because I do, you know. Every damn day." He finally turned to face me and his complexion was ruddy. Worry deepened the lines around his eyes.

"I didn't mean to upset you," I said, approaching him warily, "it's just that I'm trying to figure out when exactly the bad feelings between Sam and Nate began."

He threw up his hands in exasperation. "How the hell should I know?" he replied. "The whole team's always angry one minute, made up the next. I never heard or saw anything negative between those two until Friday afternoon. Sam got pissed and left, slamming the door behind him after I announced that I was sitting him out and giving the Ohio State game to Barnes. Nate went after him, and when I heard them arguing in the hallway, I went out to make sure things didn't escalate further. Sam was yelling at Nate about making him look bad. Said he was sure Nate was missing his passes on purpose and was catching Barnes' throws just to be spiteful. It was the stupidest thing I'd ever heard!" He shook his head, shading his eyes from the late afternoon sun. "Who would have thought he'd never play another game?"

Listening to the story of Sam's final hours through the filter of someone else's memories was more difficult than I'd thought it would be. I steadied myself to go on.

"They hadn't been fighting earlier in the week that you know of?"

"As I remember, they came to our pre-game meeting together that afternoon."

"So, it was just that disagreement that caused the tension?"

"I suppose. But why the heck does it matter now? The whole thing's water over the dam."

I stepped out of the way as a car passed between us. "It probably doesn't. I'm just trying to understand so maybe I can help Nate move on. Give life a second chance. I have one more question though, if you don't mind."

He nodded.

"It's about you. Your decision to sit Sam out..."

He rolled his eyes. "What about it?"

"It's just that I was wondering if you would have benched him if Nate hadn't caught all those passes from Zach Barnes all week?"

"What difference does it make?" he countered harshly.

I couldn't tell him why his answer was important but I needed him to be completely honest. "Maybe it won't make any difference at all, but I really need to know the truth. If Nate hadn't played so well in practice with Zach, would Sam have started in Saturday's game?"

He rubbed the back of his neck and wouldn't look me in the eye. "The truth?" He puffed his cheeks and let the air escape slowly through his teeth. "The truth is I didn't bench Sam because of Nate. I benched Sam because of Sam. He was hurt and didn't want to admit it, but it was affecting his ability to play. That's why I sat him out. So, the answer is no, it wasn't a kneejerk reaction to Nate's performance. The idea to bench him was already there. Makes me sick to think of it now." He hesitated and finally looked at me again. "Does that answer your question?"

"Yeah. It does. Thank you."

He nodded and considered me one final time before turning to leave. "You know," he called over his shoulder as he climbed into the driver's seat, "if he could get his grades up high enough to be reinstated, I would take him back in a second. He's a good ballplayer and a nice young man. It's a shame two careers got destroyed that night. Maybe you'll be able to get through to him."

I knew the chances of *getting through* to Nate were slim to none, and I was done with that dead-end tactic. I had a better strategy for getting him back on the field and back into his own life, but there were still a few details I needed to address before I was ready to commit fully to my plan.

I had decided, if I was going to go through with using my trip, I wasn't going to tell anyone I was doing it. Brooke told her parents and Charlie had as well, but I didn't see the need to worry anyone unnecessarily about something out of their control. If everything went as I intended, no one would ever have to know, particularly since I was taking extreme precautions against making their same mistakes.

As far as I was concerned, Brooke's main issues stemmed from the fact that she traveled for an extended period of time. Each time she traveled for almost six months. It was no wonder she encountered such problems when she returned. I was only going to need one day to accomplish what I was setting out to do and couldn't imagine anything catastrophic happening in less than twenty-four hours.

The side effects created by Charlie's experience weighed far more heavily on my mind. He was arrested for saving two lives, both his father's and his mother's, during his trip to the past. Both of their deaths had been prevented without Charlie's knowledge or intent and the fact that he was sentenced to fifteen years in prison despite his lack of direct intervention concerned me. Since Sam's death would occur on the date I was returning it would be imperative that I do everything in my power to assure his accident would still happen. As much as it destroyed me to know I might see him and be unable to save him, I couldn't risk saving a life - at least not that of a person who was already dead. Nate's life was another story altogether.

I came to terms with the changes I was planning for his timeline. I could only hope that keeping him from fighting with Sam would remove the guilt associated with his death. The trick would be eliminating the fight without saving Sam's life.

In any event, I consoled myself with a single comment Charlie made just after we discovered his mother saved his life. He mentioned how ironic it was that he saved lives and got arrested while Brooke's actions caused Mrs. Cooper's death and she was never discovered. With that in mind and under the guise of researching for Senator Turner, I called several members of the Time Travel Safety and Investigation Board to probe them for information regarding inconsistencies in their arrest procedures.

I discovered the TTSIB, as well as several of the other federal agencies tasked with supervising time travel, historically suffered from a severe lack of staff and funding making it necessary for them to streamline operations. Because of the shortage, protocol for monitoring individual trips was established within the first five years of public travel, thereby eliminating the burden of tracking each and every trip. Statistical analyses were recorded during those early years, documenting the types of travelers who broke the laws most frequently. The research showed highly-educated men between the ages of eighteen and forty from wealthy backgrounds were far more likely to break traveling laws than those in all the other groups combined. Based on those findings, the government used its meager resources to monitor just those travelers the analysis program deemed a threat.

I prayed being a girl would save me from being monitored just as it had saved Brooke.

I clung to that hope each day I snuck off Grounds to my mandatory time travel classes. They were boring. Uninspired. I felt as if I'd learned more in my own life about time travel than I was learning from the board-certified instructors. While I was supposed to be taking notes on significant events in time travel history, I created dozens of flowcharts tracking "what if" scenarios, playing out the full ramification of each of my possible moves. My future felt like a giant game of chess where the outcome was based solely on my first move. The first move had to be right.

While I juggled schoolwork, friendships, and my traveling classes, I also kept tabs on Nate in the event he should own up to his addiction, rendering my trip unnecessary. His oldest sister, Kay, was the most responsible of his siblings and also my strongest ally in the battle for his sobriety. We'd established something of a friendship through the course of my relationship with Nate so she didn't find it particularly odd that I should reach out to her inquiring about his well-being.

"Have you seen him lately?" I asked during our most recent conversation.

"Not since his hearing last week. I meant to call you about it, but the kids have been so busy with school starting and fall sports, I just didn't have a chance."

"It's okay," I said, unaware that his hearing had already taken place. "What happened?"

She groaned into the receiver. "The judge let him off easy. I was hoping maybe jail time would knock some sense into him, but he got off with just a fine and community service, if you can believe that. I guess I should be happy for him, but there's no way I can celebrate anything to do with the mess he's gotten himself into. He was supposed to be the one of us who did something great. So much for that."

I heard screaming in the background, like the sound of something feral.

"Do you know where he is now? What he's doing?" I asked over the din.

"Turn down that television and stop hitting your brother!" she called to one of her children. "God bless. I'm sorry. They're about to kill each other in there. Every time the phone rings it's like a signal to lose their minds. Anyway, what about Nate?"

Part of me felt sorry for bothering her. But she was my only reliable source of information. "I just asked about where he is now?"

I could hear the sound of a door being shut and the children's squawking quieted. "He's at home with Mom and Dad, although I don't know for how much longer. They're about done with him too. Mom caught him taking money out of her wallet on Tuesday. I don't know what to tell her to do. I just wish Nate would hit rock bottom and get on with it."

Instead of responding, I bit my tongue. What exactly was he supposed to get on with?

Recovery?

Normalcy?

Death?

As much as I liked Kay, I didn't agree with how she dealt with Nate's addiction. In fact, I didn't agree with how any of his family approached it, as a conscious choice, instead of what it truly was - the most visible symptom of his unresolved issues. I couldn't make them understand that he needed aggressive therapy, not condemnation, and so knowing the environment he was living in only intensified my guilt.

When I didn't respond immediately, Kay began rambling to fill the awkward silence. "He talks about you, you know? Gets nostalgic about stuff you did together. While we were waiting together for his hearing he kept repeating over and over again that you were the best person he'd ever known. He'd tell me and then five minutes later he'd tell me again, as if he'd forgotten that he already said it aloud." She paused. "You must be on his mind a lot."

I welled up, thinking about how abandoned he must have felt. I was a horrible person. "He's on my mind a lot too," I said finally.

"I gotta tell you, Melody, none of us blame you for breaking up with him. I can't believe you hung in there as long as you did to be honest. You're too young to be tied down to the train wreck he's become. You need to get out there and find someone new, you know? I mean, I don't mind talking to you and keeping you updated on how he's doing, but if you're hoping he's gonna pull out of this, I think you're wasting your time. Seriously. You should find someone who won't let you down."

I had no desire to continue our conversation. After hearing what I needed to know, that my trip was still necessary, I suddenly couldn't wait to hang up. I thanked her for her time and promised to keep in touch, but knew I wouldn't call again, especially since every word she spoke drove daggers into my heart. Her final comment about finding someone who wouldn't let me down was a hard pill to swallow. Nate wasn't the only one who disappointed people.

By November, the time had come. I scheduled my trip for the Wednesday before Thanksgiving and told my mom I was going to Lesley's house overnight to meet her family's new puppy and would be home the next day, in plenty of time to help stuff the turkey. I figured I might need extra time alone Wednesday night just in case something didn't go as planned. I was nothing if not thorough and always arranged for contingencies.

I was hoping, of course, that everything would work out perfectly so by the time I got home Thursday morning, Nate would be on his way to my house for dinner, and we would be free to live out our happily-ever-after.

Chapter Twenty-One

Fall Semester – Third Year/Second Year

The morning of my departure, I woke up early. Like 2:00 AM early. And I wasn't excited – I was petrified.

It dawned on me, as my eyes adjusted to the dark, that changing the outcome of Nate's situation wasn't going to change Nate. Regardless of whether I was able to successfully keep him from the guilt associated with Sam's death, I would never be able to remove whatever fostered his addictive tendencies from deep within. It was there, and it was a part of who he was, just waiting for the right combination of stress and pain to release it from its dormancy. It was a truth I had never fully considered.

As the paleness of morning peeked between the mini-blind slats, I stretched and yawned, still disquieted by my middle-of-the-night revelation. On my back, staring at the dingy popcorn ceiling, I did what I always did when faced with a dilemma.

I plotted the worst-case scenario.

Suppose I had to spend the rest of my life waiting for Nate to succumb to the temptation of addiction? How would it be to never know when something might trigger him to use? Could I be with a man who was a ticking time bomb of self-destruction?

In an instant I knew that I could. I wouldn't like it and it wouldn't be easy, but there were no promises in life. I couldn't guarantee that anyone I met and fell in love with wouldn't have their own laundry list of issues. Nate was kind and he was honest.

He loved and respected me, challenging me to be the very best version of myself. Perhaps having his demons out in the open would make them less sinister. Knowing what they were, I could face them and help him to deal with them, if need be, before they were allowed to take over.

It was little consolation, but it was all that I had – just enough to propel me, one foot in front of the other, through the entrance of the same time travel facility both Brooke and Charlie had passed through years before.

I had come too far. There was no turning back.

My trip wasn't scheduled until 3 PM and it took over an hour of processing before my chaperone led me to the stainless-steel chamber which would send me back to relive the most important day of my young life. Employees kept asking if I was alone or if there was someone I was waiting for – apparently most travelers brought a companion along for moral support. As I waited for the countdown to begin, the space beyond the glass wall reserved for friends and family remained empty and I knew why coming alone was discouraged. Directions were piped in through the loudspeaker, and I regretted there was no one to send me off. No one to wish me well or greet me when I returned.

As a blinding light filled the chamber, I held my breath and closed my eyes. A moment later, the brightness dimmed, and I tentatively opened one eye, peering at the scene before me, half expecting to still be in the chamber. I found, however, that I was in the old dorm room Lesley and I shared my second year. Three of her hoodies were thrown over the back of her desk chair and a pile of my books were strewn across my unmade bed, proving I had indeed been delivered to the right time and place. A quick glance at the clock confirmed she was still in her 10:30 chemistry class, assuring she wouldn't come looking for me until lunchtime. I tore a piece of notebook paper from the folder on her desk and jotted a quick note to inform her of my whereabouts. Without wasting another second,

I set out in pursuit of Nate. If my plan was going to work, I knew I needed to move quickly.

On Fridays, Nate took Great Civilizations of the Western World at eight o'clock and Spanish at 9:20. I had absolutely no idea what he did after class on this particular day because in the original timeline I spent the morning by myself, studying in the library with a hot cup of coffee and my favorite playlist. Wherever he was and whatever he was doing, I hoped he was willing to change his plans. I sent him a quick text.

Over these case files. But they gave me a crazy idea. Wanna blow off the rest of the day with me?

I hurried beneath the canopy of ancient oaks that lined The Lawn, a huge grassy knoll situated between the dorms and the main Grounds as I waited for him to reply. I was giddy at the prospect of being face to face with him again. It had been months since I'd seen or spoken to him and over a year since we'd shared anything that resembled a normal conversation. Nate – the old Nate, my Nate, was somewhere on Grounds wholly unaware of what his life was about to become. Of what our life was about to become. At that moment, waiting on the cusp, I decided that if I got nothing more out of my trip than one more amazing afternoon with him, it might just be enough.

Beads of sweat broke out on my forehead, and I remembered just how hot it had been those first weeks back. Having taken the weather into consideration when I formulated my plan, I hoped the scorching temperatures would make my proposal an easy sell. As I rolled the sleeves of my t-shirt, my phone buzzed in my pocket.

Thought it was just u and ur books this morning ☺, he replied.

The anticipation of having him so close was almost too much to bear.

Change of heart. Someone wise said life wasn't worth living if it wasn't fun. Hotter today than yesterday. Maybe we should go get wet.

Within seconds, he responded.

I like where this is headed. Whatcha got in mind?

149

My hands shook as my fingers flew across the keys.

Tubing? James River? U'd have to blow off practice...

I pressed send and waited. My entire trip hinged on whether or not I would be able to persuade him to skip practice. It wasn't something I'd seen him do – in fact, he was more likely to play injured or with a fever than not show up. I was about to send another message when his reply appeared.

First game of the season tomorrow. Don't know if I should bail. Coach would probably bench me.

My chest tightened involuntarily. Although I fully expected him to push back, I was still strangely disappointed when he did. I immediately began typing the response I'd already prepared.

So come up with a good excuse not to be there. When ur 40 and ur remembering this day, what do u think you'll actually remember – practice or tubing with me?

I recycled a line he'd used on me in the past, and I could picture him weighing his options, his forehead wrinkled up as it always did when he was faced with a decision. I moved into the shade of a nearby building and sat on the front step, praying I'd gotten through to him while I considered my next move. I watched students as they passed, without a legitimate care in the world. Little did they know about Sam's impending accident or the loss we would collectively endure. I felt a pang of regret knowing I hadn't scheduled time to see Sam while I was back. I'd been so intent on assuring he would make the same mistake twice, I hadn't considered the possibility of a proper goodbye. My phone remained silent in my hands as I quickly convinced myself that avoiding Sam was for the best. The less I changed the timeline, the better off everyone would be.

My phone buzzed, startling me from my thoughts. I nervously peered at the screen.

Get ur suit. Be at the parking lot in 20 minutes. If this ruins my shot at the NFL, ur toast.

Joy exploded from every pore of my body as I leapt from the step and raced back to my room. Consequences be damned, I was spending the afternoon with Nate.

He was already waiting for me, sitting in his 4Runner with the windows open as the blacktop threatened to burn my feet through the bottom of my well-worn flip flops. He looked up, grinning widely as he heard me approach.

"The student becomes the teacher, is that it?" he asked as I slid into the seat beside him.

"Something like that," I replied, mesmerized by the unbelievable change in his appearance and demeanor. Having not yet experienced the grief of Sam's death or subsequent addiction, he was almost unrecognizable without the dark circles, bleary, red eyes, and torment casting a constant shadow over his complexion. In front of me was the man I'd fallen in love with; a man who was ready to throw caution to the wind and live life on all cylinders.

He started the engine and headed off Grounds. "How'd you come up with this crazy idea?" he asked. "It's seriously out of character, especially when there's work to be done," he added, his voice raising an octave as he attempted a rather weak impersonation of me.

"Ha, ha," I said resting my feet on his dashboard. It was strange for him to be driving since I had served as his designated driver for so many months. I savored the simple pleasure of being chauffeured. "As a matter of fact, I was reading about the history of lawmaking, dating back to the forefathers and Jefferson kept coming up over and over again, and that made me think of Monticello and what a good time we had when we visited there last Christmas. I thought about how cold it was that day and how hot it was yesterday and that the only good thing to do on days like this is go swimming. But of course, we don't have a pool, so I tried to figure out where we could go swimming and that made me think of the river and how much fun it would be to go tubing."

He turned his attention from the road and wagged his finger at me. "Your head is a weird place. A good place, but weird, nevertheless." He returned to his driving and began lecturing me in a voice he reserved for his brothers. "You wanna know what I told the coach to get out of practice?" he asked, continuing without waiting for me to respond. "I told him I ate something bad at breakfast and had explosive diarrhea. Explosive diarrhea! That's the best I could come up with. Told him there was no way I could make it to practice in my condition and that I was going to rest up so I could be ready for the game tomorrow." He feigned anger but was having trouble keeping a straight face. He was a horrible actor. "You better hope and pray that we don't see anyone from school this afternoon or I'm screwed. Totally screwed. And it will be *all* your fault."

"You didn't have to come," I replied glibly, tossing my hair in his direction as I pretended to pout. "You just can't resist the promise of good time."

He wove his hand beneath my hair and gently squeezed the back of my neck. "My trouble is that I just can't resist you," he countered. "I think I would actually succumb to explosive diarrhea if it meant getting to spend the day with you."

My heart melted inside my chest. What a delight it was to hear him fawn over me the way he had before the accident instead of bickering with me about how horrible his life had become.

To be adored was one of life's most cherished gifts.

"Do you really think I'd let you?" I teased.

"Let me what?"

"Let you spend the day with me if you had explosive diarrhea?"

He turned on his blinker and merged into the left-hand lane. "I honestly think you would. If I was sick, you'd take care of me. If I needed you, you'd be there. Even if I did have explosive diarrhea."

I blanched. Here he was, trusting me to be there for him, believing that I'd always be there to help if he needed me. I hadn't always been that person for him, but it confirmed that using my trip was the right thing to do.

It was a forty-minute ride south to James River Runners. Along the way Nate chatted mindlessly about the ungodly number of papers his biology teacher assigned and what an idiot the TA in his biomechanics class was. Listening to him pontificate about school instead of watching him nod off was so refreshing that it didn't dawn on me to offer up my own opinions or even elaborate when he asked about my classes. Instead, I forced myself to enjoy being present in the moment, knowing there was no guarantee I wouldn't return to the same ailing Nate I left behind.

We picked up lunch at Subway about a mile from the river, and as we sat eating our subs on the curb outside the restaurant, I broached the topic of football. Nate was the only person I hadn't interviewed about what transpired in the days before the accident. And although it was too late to alter my course based on his response, I couldn't stop myself from asking.

"Are you excited about the first game tomorrow?"

"Yeah. I'm ready. I'm not sure Sam is though."

I picked up a bit of shredded lettuce that had fallen onto my lap and popped it into my mouth. "Oh really? Why not?" I asked, pretending not to know about the coach practicing Barnes.

He swallowed, washing down a bite of sandwich with his soda. "It's weird. He hasn't been himself on the field since we got back to school. I don't know if something's bothering him outside of football or if his arm is still hurting him from his fall at the quarry, but his passing game's been awful and I don't know how to help..." He trailed off, watching a group of vultures circling in the sky above our heads.

"Did you ask him about it?"

"Yeah. I mean I tried. I can't be all, 'Hey, Sam, why are you throwing like a middle-schooler?' can I? I tried asking him about his wrist, but he just blows me off. I did see him in with the trainer last week so maybe he's finally ready to admit it's really hurt." He crumpled up his wrapper and tossed it into the bag. "All I know is it's gonna be a rough game tomorrow if he doesn't figure something out fast."

Sweat pooled on my nape and I twirled my hair into a messy bun to get it off my neck. I was dying to know if Nate was aware of the coach's plan to sit Sam out. I almost didn't ask but couldn't stop myself.

"You don't think Coach would put Barnes in, do you?"

"Who knows. Maybe. Coach had him running plays with the offensive line all week so I'd say it's a possibility." He pulled open his bag of chips and shoved several in his mouth. "I hope he doesn't bench Sam though. He'd rather die."

If he'd been looking at me instead of his chips, Nate would have seen my inexorable, visceral reaction to the mention of Sam's death — a death I alone was aware of. Just hearing his name used in that context brought back the painful memories of his passing and it was all I could do to keep from tearing up.

"Well," I said, attempting to regain my composure, "I'm sure whatever the coach decides will be in the best interest of the team, and all of you need to be adult enough to accept those decisions."

Nate stopped munching to stare at me. "Sometimes it's like I don't even know you," he whispered. "I mean, where do you come up with this stuff?" He made the 'cuckoo' sign and pointed. "You're a strange duck."

"You're a strange duck!" I countered, throwing my balled-up sub wrapper at his head. "I'm just saying that whatever happens, it won't be anyone's fault."

He finished off the last of his lunch and stood up to take our trash to the bin. "If Coach benches him, it'll be Sam's fault for not proving he's worthy of suiting up tomorrow. The best guys play and everyone knows it. You don't perform, you don't play. I just hope to God Sam gets his stuff worked out in time to have a good run this season. I don't know if Barnes can carry us to a winning record."

Nate took my hand as we walked back to the truck, the same way he always did, with my fingers tucked inside his. The security of his embrace, without the familiar dampness or shaking, filled me with a sudden desperation – a longing for a return to this Nate, this relationship, this life. Since before lunch, I had almost forgotten what I was experiencing was only borrowed time, and that in less than twenty-four hours I'd be returned to the reality of my life.

A life that I hoped would be reset to undo the tragedy of Nate's addiction.

We spent the entire afternoon floating along the refreshing waters of the James River, lounging atop large inflatable inner tubes from the drop off point back to Hatton Ferry. We talked and splashed and hopped out to explore Fallsburg Creek and Goosby Island, even though we'd been warned against it. After throwing our tubes on the bank, we scampered into the woods, chasing each other like children through the brush. In the center of the island was a clearing, just thin enough for the sun to break through, drying our suits against our skin. Nate gathered me into his arms, pressing his cool chest against my cheek. I could hear the quickness of his heart.

"This may have been the very best idea you've ever had," he murmured.

The weight of his admission wasn't lost on me. "I hope so," I replied, knowing just how much our future hinged upon the strength of my plan.

He twirled a damp strand of my hair around his fingers. "Maybe I should just give up football altogether and waste all my time hanging out with you."

I peered up at him. "One good idea does not a pattern make, Nate. There's no telling when I'll come up with another one. It could be weeks. Months. Years even. Think of all the fun you'd miss on the field waiting for me to figure something out." He grinned at me, his eyes dancing. "Seriously, just stick with football. I can't handle that sort of pressure."

"Have it your way," he said, as he let his fingers explore the edges of my bikini top. "I can wait."

He kissed me then for the first time all day, and I was overwhelmed by the sheer passion of his touch. Every kiss since Sam's death had been tainted by his grief – dull and lifeless, given only to maintain the pretense of our bond. But this kiss... this kiss was different. This kiss reminded me I wasn't only loved, I was cherished.

In that moment, I decided using my trip was worth it, regardless of the consequences on the other side. To have Nate, the real Nate, back in my arms again was a delicious indulgence worth savoring. It wasn't long before we were a sweaty tangle of limbs and bodies, entwined together on a blanket of soft earth.

We emerged from the woods, flushed and stained with mud, to find our inner tubes right where we'd left them on the bank of the river. Grinning at each other, we scrubbed our knees and elbows in the fresh water and paddled back toward the main channel. The sun was getting low and we knew we were at risk of incurring a late charge if we weren't back to the rafting outfit by 7 PM.

As amazing as our day together was, I couldn't keep my anxiety at bay as we drove back to school. I had trouble holding myself together, knowing in a few hours Sam would either accidentally kill himself or he wouldn't. If he didn't, then I faced potential imprisonment when I returned. And if he did, then I knew Nate was going to lose his best friend again. I just hoped this time I wasn't going to lose Nate too.

We decided not to chance running into anyone on Grounds, and after a late dinner on the far side of town, snuck into Nate's apartment without being seen. We holed up in his room together playing video games, and while Nate slept soundly in his bed beside me, I laid awake, wondering how long it would take for news of the accident to reach him without my eyewitness account. I saw the clock change to one and then to two. Still, no phone call came. Returning home after a night of partying, students milled around outside the building, rowdy and obnoxious, but with no news of the crash.

When morning arrived and there were still no messages or calls, I started freaking out. I tiptoed into the hallway to check for news of the accident on my phone but was devastated not to find a single mention of Sam or a late-night crash.

At six o'clock I roused Nate just enough to let him know I was walking to my dorm room for a change of clothes. I kissed him tenderly on the cheek and said goodbye, already resigning myself to the possibility of punishment upon my return. I needed to be alone for my transfer back to the present and as much as it destroyed me to leave him behind, I tearfully acknowledged I had accomplished everything I set out to do. There was nothing left but to pray.

I found a secluded classroom on the first floor of Monroe Hall and closed the door behind me to await the transfer. Crouching on the floor out of sight in the corner of the room, I rocked on my heels and willed myself not to cry.

Moments before the transfer my phone buzzed. I ignored it briefly, assuming it was Nate asking me to return, but at the last second, I decided to see who it was.

And then came the blinding light.

Part Two

Fall Semester — Third Year

Chapter Twenty-Two

⬥◦◦◇◦◦⬥◦◦◇◦◦⬥

I expected officers to be waiting for me at the door of the chamber, but when the hydraulic locks disengaged and the door slid open, I was shocked to discover I was alone. There were arrows on the linoleum tiles directing me toward the facility's exit, and I stopped briefly at the security office to sign off on the registry, indicating I'd returned from my trip.

"You enjoy yourself?" the security officer asked as I set down the pen.

"Uh, yeah. I had a nice time. Thanks," I replied, anxious to get away before anyone changed their minds about arresting me. I threw on my coat and without another word, headed for the exit.

"Miss Johnson?" he called after me as the sliding doors opened.

For a split second I considered ignoring him, pretending I hadn't heard my name. I contemplated making a run for my car since he couldn't arrest me if he couldn't catch me.

I would go on the run. Live off the land. Disappear until the government forgot who I was.

"Have a great Thanksgiving!" he said finally when I didn't respond.

I exhaled. "You too," I replied thinly as I hurried out the door.

It was a good thing the drive from the facility to the motel where I intended to hole up for the night was a familiar route because I could barely concentrate on my driving along the way. In addition to checking my rearview mirror for flashing lights, I'd underestimated the stress associated with not knowing how a full year of my life had played out. For the first time I acknowledged that along with helping Nate, the other consequence of a successful trip was an entire year's worth of experiences I'd be unable to recall. If Sam's death hadn't affected Nate as profoundly as it did the first time and he hadn't started taking pills, it stood to reason that he and I would have spent more time together doing the things we typically did.

He would remember all of it.

And I wouldn't remember a thing.

Still, more terrifying than facing a life without memories of the past year was acknowledging the possibility that my plan hadn't worked at all. That keeping Nate from fighting with Sam hadn't been enough to spare him the guilt associated with his death. If that was the case, our day together on the James River would be our last.

I spent a restless night at a roach motel just outside town and wasted no time heading home in the morning. A tiny part of me expected to be greeted by a squadron of police cruisers, but when I pulled up to the house, the only car in the driveway was my mom's. I lugged my suitcase out of the trunk and let myself in through the front door.

"Mom?" I called as I hung my coat in the hall closet.

"I'm in the kitchen," she replied. "You're just in time to help peel potatoes."

I left my belongings at the foot of the stairs and joined my mother in front of the stove. Her presence paired with the sight of her familiar preparations helped ease my nerves at once.

"It smells delicious already," I told her, placing a kiss on her cheek. I took a deep breath, not only to savor the aroma of the roasting turkey, but also as a means of composing myself for the conversation I was about to have. It was time to find out what I'd missed.

"You said you need these potatoes peeled?"

"I do," she replied. "They've already been scrubbed. Just grab the peeler from the drawer."

I crossed over to the sink to wash my hands before starting on the potatoes. "About how many of these do you think we'll need?" I asked nonchalantly, hoping to discern who was coming for dinner.

"I don't think we'll need too many. It will be just us since Grandma and Uncle Brad's family aren't coming. I understand why they want to be with Cheryl's family though," she remarked.

"Oh," I replied, remembering Cheryl's father's illness. "When is everyone else getting here?"

She sliced the last of the crust off a stack of bread for the stuffing and glanced at her watch. "Brooke and Charlie should be here in about an hour. And you never did get back to me about what time Nate was coming. I assume you told him we're eating at one o'clock?"

I steadied myself against the sink, suddenly needing it for support. Nate was coming to Thanksgiving dinner. At my house. And this was normal.

"I'm sure I did," I breathed, overwhelmed by the promise of a reunion. "Maybe I should text him just to be sure."

Mom scoffed. "You haven't been apart for twenty-four hours and you're already looking for an excuse to call that boy. I swear with you two it's like Charlie and Brooke all over again. It wouldn't kill you to give each other a little space. I couldn't believe you actually left him long enough to go to Lesley's last night." She wiped her hands on her 'Gobble 'Til You Wobble' apron. "How was that by the way?"

I turned from her and stared out the window into the back yard, collecting my thoughts as I watched a squirrel gathering acorns at the base of a sprawling oak. If Nate and I had been together at school the day before, it was a relief to know my trip had achieved some level of success. Hopefully he was still attending classes because he had never been kicked out.

With regard to Lesley, I had no idea how to respond since I had never actually gone to her house in either timeline. I could never tell my mom I'd lied to her about using my trip as it would devastate her to know the risk I'd taken, so I gave her just enough information to satisfy her curiosity.

"It was fine. The puppy's adorable. Her family sends their hellos." I placed the peeler beside the sink and dried my hands on a towel before pulling my phone from my pocket to send Nate a text.

Hi. Eating at 1. Will u be here by then?

His reply came through several minutes later.

Finally stopped at a light. U told me 10 times not 2 b late. Only 15 minutes out. CU soon.

My heart flip-flopped and so did my stomach. The fact that he was driving to my house on his own was a good indication he was sober. The fact he was on time, even more so. I smiled to myself, thinking how I must have harassed him about being early, knowing I would want to get answers to my questions about our time apart sooner than later. I couldn't believe in fifteen minutes I would know for sure if my trip back in time was a success.

"Good news," I told Mom. "You're gonna get some extra help with dinner. He's almost here."

She dumped another loaf of bread onto the counter and began cutting it into cubes. "Why don't you run upstairs and make sure there are towels in the guest bath and an extra blanket on Charlie's bed before Nate gets here. Then you two can finish the potatoes."

I had just unearthed a spare blanket in the linen closet when the doorbell rang. I sprinted down the stairs and nearly tackled my mom on her way through the foyer.

"Good grief!" she exclaimed, backing away from the door. "It's like you haven't seen him in a month!"

I couldn't explain that my zealous behavior was completely warranted given our estrangement in the original timeline. And although I was acting no saner than a hormone-fueled teenager, my excitement could not be restrained as I threw open the door.

"Long time no see," Nate said as he slid past me with his bag and a large bouquet of flowers he immediately handed to my mom.

"Oh, Nate, thank you!" she gushed, lifting the blooms beneath her nose. "They're divine."

He tossed his bag on the floor and took off his coat. "It's my pleasure, Mrs. Johnson. It was nice of you to invite me since we didn't end up having a game over the holiday. I just wish there was more I could do to say thanks."

"Well, there's lots you can do," she laughed, taking him by the arm. "In fact, there's a whole kitchen full of food that needs preparing!"

Mom led him to the back of the house and I tagged along behind, overwhelmed by my good fortune. It appeared my trip to the past had produced the desired effect. Nate was back in school, back on the team, and no longer addicted to pills. I could only assume, since I had not yet been arrested, that Sam had died in the new timeline just as he had originally. Either that or he was still alive and my trip hadn't been monitored. It would take some constructive prying to discover which was the case.

I returned to the potatoes and listened to my mom and Nate making small talk. I figured it was best to keep my mouth shut until I had a clearer picture of what had happened in the fourteen months since I'd altered the timeline. They chatted about the team's losing season and how Barnes still wasn't making the cut as their first-string quarterback. I initially deduced from his comment Barnes was playing because of Sam's death, but remembered that regardless of what had happened, Sam would no longer be on the team. Even if he was alive, he would have graduated last May.

Mom grilled him about his classes while he peeled and sliced beside me at the sink. He rubbed against my shoulder as we fought for the same space and the pleasure of having him so close was almost more than I could stand. I could smell his deodorant, crisp and fresh and familiar, and I was suddenly envious of the Melody who got to stay with him the day after our tubing trip and all the days after while I was stuck living the nightmare of the original timeline. For a moment, I was sad. Jealous. Angry. And then he kissed me

165

softly on the top of my head, pulling me from my negative thoughts and just like that, I wasn't disappointed any more. Nate was back and everything was going to be okay.

We finished combining the ingredients of the green bean casserole and Nate was placing it in the oven when I heard footsteps coming from the front of the house.

"Hello?" Charlie called. "Anybody home?"

"Me," I replied from inside the refrigerator where I was searching for the fresh cranberry sauce. "We're all back here."

My brother appeared in the kitchen, flushed from the outdoors with Brooke by his side.

"My parents are right behind us," Brooke announced, collapsing onto a stool at the counter. "They forgot the wine and went back home to get it."

I shut the refrigerator door and set the cranberries on the table. Excited by the prospect of sharing Vicki's first Thanksgiving with everyone I loved, I peeked around the counter for her car seat but was disappointed to see it wasn't there.

"Where's my chicklet?" I asked.

Charlie nodded in the direction of the foyer. "Sleeping. Little booger had us up all night. I should be the one passed out cold."

"I'm gonna go take a peek anyway," I squealed, curious to see how much she'd grown since my last visit home. "I promise to be quiet."

I tiptoed through the hallway into the foyer where I spotted her car seat against the far wall. I approached the sleeping infant and carefully adjusted the blanket so I could see her precious face.

But the child in the car seat wasn't Vicki. In fact, whoever it was wasn't even a girl.

A plump baby boy slept soundly - a teddy bear hat covered his oversized head and fire engine pacifier was tucked between his lips.

I reached down to brush his cheek and the truth of his existence brought me to my knees.

Although my trip back in time succeeded in freeing Nate from his demons, somehow my niece had become collateral damage and no longer existed in the augmented timeline. Instead there was a nephew. Whatever happened in the twenty-four hours I was gone replaced the child who stole my heart with one I had never met.

I struggled to breathe. Certain I was dreaming, I willed myself to wake up, opening and closing my eyes repeatedly only to gaze down upon the same unfamiliar child. A child who was not my Vicki.

"You okay?" Nate whispered from the hallway. His stealthy arrival startled me and I immediately turned away, knowing I was in no condition to face him or the family waiting for me in the kitchen. I couldn't let on that the baby had upset me for fear of giving myself away.

"I'm not feeling well all of a sudden," I explained, making my way to the staircase. "I think I'm just going to go upstairs and lay down for a couple minutes. I'll be down in a bit, okay?"

He took several steps in my direction. "You don't look so hot, Mel. You want me to send your mom up?"

The room began to spin and I grabbed the railing with both hands to keep from falling over. "No!" I replied a little too forcefully. "I'm fine. I just need a few minutes to myself."

He rushed to my side, taking me under the arm. "What's wrong? Are you sick?" he asked.

I yanked free of his grasp and forced myself to continue climbing. "Ten minutes. Just give me ten minutes. Please," I begged. "I just need to be alone."

Nate relented, but I could feel him watching me as I continued making my way up the steps.

How could I tell him I'd unknowingly sacrificed Vicki's life for his? How could I tell him I'd changed my world and nothing would ever be the same again?

Chapter Twenty-Three

⬦•◽•◇•◽•⬦•◽•◇•◽•⬦

Alone in my room, I shut the door behind me and fought to control my emotions. I knew someone would be up to check on me shortly so there'd be very little time to collect my thoughts.

Vicki's disappearance overshadowed the thrill of Nate's return as I began to unravel how the changes I made to my own timeline might have resulted in her replacement. I pulled out my tablet and found an app to calculate the approximate date of her conception given her premature birth.

Sure enough, the day of my trip fell within the window of her conception.

For several minutes I sat in dumbfounded silence trying to figure out how anything I did during my trip could have had any bearing on Vicki's conception. And then I remembered the call I made to Charlie while Nate and I waited at the hospital after Sam's accident in the original timeline. I'd forgotten to call during my trip so perhaps without my brief interruption, the course of his evening changed just enough so that instead of conceiving Vicki, Brooke and Charlie's DNA combined instead to form a different tiny person – the baby boy sleeping in the car seat downstairs.

Chromosomes realigned. Everything changed. Just. Like. That.

Vicki was gone forever, and I was the only one who knew.

The reality of this burden rested heavily upon my shoulders, but I knew for everyone else's sake I needed to pull myself together. They were blissfully unaware that in another time and place there was a

169

daughter. A beautiful little girl with a head of wispy auburn hair and a gummy grin that made all your troubles melt away. She ceased to exist the moment I reset the timeline with my trip and although I was going to miss her terribly, I knew there was no reason to complicate my family's lives with the knowledge of her absence or my journey.

I would have to put my memories of Vicki in a box on a shelf and pretend I'd never known her. I would have to grow to love my new nephew and put aside my love for my niece.

And as hard as it was going to be, I would need to keep my sadness to myself.

A quiet rap on the door roused me from my thoughts and I wondered which one of my family had drawn the short straw.

"Come in," I breathed.

Charlie appeared in the doorway with my nephew on his hip. The baby's eyes were bloodshot, pooled with tiny tears.

"I'm so sorry," I said, sliding to make room for him to sit beside me on the bed. "Did I wake him?"

He carried the newest member of my family over to me and placed him on my lap. I felt terrible. I didn't even know his name.

"Nah. You know Mikey. He never sleeps. I think he's taken fifteen years off my life already."

My nephew's name was Mikey. I assumed it was actually Michael, probably after my great-grandfather. I glanced down at the grumpy butterball perched on my knee and squelched my resentment.

"Still, I'm sorry. I didn't mean to cause trouble." I coughed nervously, trying to ignore how awkward Mikey seemed in my arms, so different from the ease I'd always felt with Vicki. He squirmed and began to whimper, almost as if he sensed my discomfort.

"What's gotten into you, fussypants?" Charlie scolded, scooping the baby off my lap. "It's just Aunt Mel, silly boy!" He held Mikey above his face and blew raspberries onto his tummy, eliciting squeals of delight. When the baby finally settled down, Charlie propped him back on his hip and turned his attention to me.

"Nate said you weren't feeling well. I just wanted to make sure you were okay." He eyed me suspiciously, raising one eyebrow. "Are you trying to get out of cleanup?"

I shook my head to avoid looking directly at him. "No. I've just been getting these dizzy spells," I lied, standing up from the bed. "I'm fine now. Probably just low blood sugar. I should come down and eat." I took a step toward the door but Charlie didn't move.

"Are you sure that's it?" he asked. "Nate seemed to think there might be something more."

I waved him off. "He's a serious over-reactor. I'm fine. Really." I couldn't tell him what had happened to his baby daughter. I couldn't.

I wouldn't.

He reluctantly followed me into the hallway.

Back downstairs, I evaded unnecessary conversation to keep from raising suspicions about my behavior as well as to avoid accidentally saying something about Vicki or the unknown portions of my timeline. It was difficult not to dwell upon the reality of what I'd done, but I found that I was eventually able to focus on listening to the others. Curled up in Nate's arms on the sofa watching the football game on TV, I began filling in the missing pieces of my life.

I learned that unlike Vicki, Mikey had gone full-term and had been born as anticipated in the middle of June. As slight in stature as Vicki had been, Mikey was quite the opposite - a stocky, strapping, armful of a child with the disposition to match. He cried through most of dinner and we were all quite relieved when he passed out cold on the family room floor just before dessert.

With regard to my own life, I was happy to discover I'd taken the same classes during the spring semester ensuring I hadn't fallen behind in my studies. And since Mikey's timely arrival gave Brooke plenty of maternity leave, I'd spent the summer working full-time with Senator Turner instead of babysitting for Brooke and Charlie. I made a mental note to follow up on the specifics of our collaboration since I assumed I would be working for her again next summer.

Of course, the best change was Nate's transformation from riddled addict back to fun-loving boyfriend. After everyone headed home for the night, we found ourselves alone in the kitchen, cleaning up the last of the dishes.

"Is it weird not to be preparing for a game tomorrow?" I asked, passing him a clean platter from the sudsy sink.

"Yeah. Sort of." He plucked the dishtowel off his shoulder and began to dry. "Nothing's really been the same since Sam, ya know? I've seen how some teams are able to come together and play even harder to honor their fallen teammate, but we just can't get it right. There's still this black cloud hanging over our heads. It's like a funk we can't shake." He took another clean plate from my hands as the relief of knowing I hadn't prevented Sam's death washed over me. "If you wanna know the truth, I think I had more fun being here today. I can't believe I'm saying that since your family's so..."

"Amazing?" I interrupted, glaring at him from my post at the sink.

He swatted me on the rear with his towel. "That's not exactly what I was going to say," he laughed. "Amazing's pushing it. I'd say they're a little crazy. And sometimes boring, which you have to admit is true because seriously, if I had to listen to one more story from Brooke's dad about the deficit today I swear I was going to lose it. I never wanted for there to be a kids' table so bad in my entire life. That's the problem with small families you know – no kids' table."

I handed him another bowl. "Well then next year we can set up a kids' table just for you. And Mikey. How's that sound?"

He grimaced. "Ooh. Tough call. Deficit conversation or constant screaming? Maybe we should do Thanksgiving with my family next year."

Considering how difficult Mikey had been all day, it wasn't a bad suggestion. He was so different from Vicki, with her sweet, gentle disposition. I hoped perhaps we'd just caught him on a bad day.

"Maybe he'll be better by Christmas," I offered.

Nate raised a heavy stack of plates into the cabinet. "Which one? Brooke's dad or Mikey? Because I don't think either of them are changing any time soon. Mikey's been a mess every time I've seen him, and Brooke's dad is the best cure for insomnia around. Remember last summer at the beach when he tried to teach us all one hundred and one ways to tie off a fishing lure?"

I didn't remember. I hadn't been there. It made me anxious to think about all the experiences he shared with the other Melody, so before he could continue his solo trip down memory lane, I quickly changed the subject.

"I think we're almost finished cleaning up and Mom's already gone upstairs. Maybe we could pop some popcorn and see if there's a good movie on TV."

Nate tossed his dishtowel on the counter and sidled up behind me, swallowing my shoulders with his embrace.

"I thought maybe you'd want to go to bed early tonight, especially with how sick you were feeling earlier." He rested his chin on the top of my head. "What was that all about anyway?"

I was hoping he'd forgotten about my episode in the foyer, and I tucked my chin to my chest, relieved he couldn't see my face. I would have trouble lying to him if I had to look him in the eye.

"It was just a dizzy spell. Low blood sugar, that's all. I've been fine ever since."

He released his grip and spun me around, a mix of concern and mild amusement on his face.

"You know how I love playing cards with you because I can always tell what's in your hand? It's because you're a bad liar, Mel." He lifted my chin and forced me to look into his pewter eyes. "When I walked in on you and Mikey this afternoon, you looked horrified. Like you'd seen a ghost or something."

He didn't know how close to the truth he actually was. I focused my attention on a portrait of my family on the wall behind his head.

"Mel?"

173

AMALIE JAHN

I couldn't tell him about my trip and the damage I'd caused, especially when I had just saved him from the guilt associated with Sam's death. There was no way I was going to tie him to another loss.

I took a deep breath and held my cards close, praying my phony explanation would not only be believable but would also appease him.

"When I saw Mikey today, there was something in his face that reminded me of my father. I guess he's starting to resemble him a little bit. When I noticed, it just dredged up some bad memories, that's all. I just needed a minute to sort it out without ruining the day for everyone else."

"That sleeping pork chop reminded you of your father?" he asked skeptically.

"Yes."

"And so that's what it was? Bad memories of your dad?"

"Yes."

He rubbed his hands against the stubble on his cheeks and I could tell he wanted to believe me.

"And now you want to pop popcorn and veg out in front of the TV all night?"

I knew I had him.

"Yes."

He hesitated briefly. "Fine. I'm in, but only if you guys still have that powdered cheddar cheese to pour on top."

I couldn't help feeling proud of myself. Another crisis averted.

"If we have it, it's in the top cabinet. You'll have to dig for it cuz I can't reach it without a chair."

Three hours and four bowls of cheesy popcorn later, a light from the hallway sliced through the darkness and my mom appeared in her nightgown to announce she was going to bed and that she hoped we'd consider doing the same before it got too late. She had big plans for us to drive with her to the tree farm first thing in the morning to select the Johnson Family Christmas Tree. If being a part of my family's annual tradition didn't scare Nate away, nothing would.

An hour later, after Mom's final warning about sleeping in our respective rooms, I crept out of Charlie's old bedroom where Nate always stayed and slipped beneath the covers of my own bed. I assumed I would fall asleep immediately, as exhausted as I was from the excitement of the day, but instead sleep eluded me.

Vicki's disappearance plagued my mind.

I never believed myself a selfish person, but while reflecting on the aftermath of my trip and the pain of losing Vicki, I laid awake reconsidering my true intentions. Although using my trip initially stemmed from the desire to help Nate rectify what he could not remedy himself, in light of Vicki's disappearance, I could no longer pretend there hadn't been ulterior motives. I might have been able to delude myself into believing my motivations were pure if there had been no consequence for my actions, but the truth was, fixing Nate's timeline had always been just as much about fixing my own.

I wanted us to be together.

And I lost my niece in the process.

Alone, in the silent hours just before morning, I allowed myself to cry for the little girl who would never lose her first tooth or ride a bike or learn long division or fall in love. She would never become the person she was supposed to be and it was all my fault.

The last thought I had before finally drifting off to sleep was of the other lives who were lost to time travel. Vicki couldn't be the only soul whose future had been inadvertently erased at conception because of poor timing.

Perhaps, I thought, as I closed my eyes, *it was too late to save my Vicki. But maybe I could make sure no one else would ever have to experience my grief.*

Chapter Twenty-Four

———◇◇◇◇———

Returning to school with Nate for the final push before Christmas break was nothing short of miraculous. More than just company at lunchtime or someone to beat at video games, he was my best friend - the person who got me when I didn't get myself. My Nate was back, and for the first few weeks, I could not have been more thrilled. Gone was the lying, the stealing, the sneaking around for his next fix to deaden the pain. All the symptoms of his addiction had seemingly disappeared, and for a little while it was almost as if the nightmare had never even happened.

And yet, as overjoyed as I was to have the old Nate back by my side, by the time final exams rolled around, I could no longer ignore the nagging voice in the back of my mind constantly chastising me for my hasty, self-serving decision. I knew he was clean and sober not because he'd grown from that place of painful isolation and despair, but because I'd simply found a way around the difficult fix. I got what I wanted but it came at a price. Nate had no idea what monsters lay dormant within him, and I had robbed him of the satisfaction that comes along with not only facing your own demons but defeating them soundly and emerging victorious on the other side. For better or worse, I had changed who he was supposed to be.

As I zoned out during class each day considering the two lives I irrevocably changed, I found that even if I couldn't rationalize, I could at least make peace with what I did to Nate. Although I stole what may have been the defining experience of his life, I replaced it with a joyful, meaningful existence.

On the other hand, I could not forgive myself so easily for what I'd done to Vicki.

I moved quickly through the typical stages of grief, and after the initial shock wore off, lost myself briefly in the pain and guilt associated with her loss. Standing face to face with the truth of what I'd done, it was easy to understand how Nate got himself mired in the seemingly unbearable anguish which often accompanies the death of a loved one.

There was a day when taking a pill to make it all go away didn't seem like such a bad idea. But for me, that was the moment the anger set in.

And before long that anger began to fuel an obsession.

Mom noticed it immediately when I showed up for winter break dressed in crusty sweatpants and one of Nate's hoodies, grumbling as I came through the door.

"You look like you've been run over by a bus," she commented as I dropped my duffle beside the sofa where she was stretched out watching *It's a Wonderful Life* for the nine hundredth time. "You said you didn't think finals were going to be that tough."

I plopped down on the couch beside her, tucking my legs beneath me. "The tests were fine. That's not what's bothering me."

Without having to say another word, she muted the television and gave me her attention.

"You wanna talk about it now or would you rather go upstairs and get unpacked first?"

I pulled my hands into the sleeves of Nate's oversized sweatshirt, feeling very much like a child playing dress up in a grownup's clothes. Only weeks before I'd considered myself an adult – a person who made smart decisions based on careful thought and logic. Since returning from my trip however, I couldn't shake the feeling that I'd only been pretending. I made a childish, hasty decision, and although

I took full responsibility for my own actions, I was also outraged that the government enabled me to do it.

"I've been thinking a lot about time travel," I began.

"You know how we all feel," she interrupted, "so you better not be asking about using your trip."

My face flushed involuntarily and I hoped she wouldn't notice.

"No. Of course not," I stammered. "It's actually just the opposite. I was just thinking that time travel does so much more harm than good, and I don't know why we're still using such dangerous technology. I mean, think about just our family's experiences. Brooke's changes caused Mrs. Cooper's death and her parents' divorce. Charlie landed himself in prison for half his life. It's a miracle they didn't ruin everything."

She took a sip of hot tea from her *World's Best Mom* mug and considered me thoughtfully. "We all lucked out, for sure. Time travel is terribly unpredictable."

"People are terribly unpredictable. That's why I can't figure out why they let young people travel. Most eighteen-year-olds seem awfully immature to have that sort of power, especially over other people's lives."

Mom shook her head. "Young people don't hold the monopoly on bad decisions. Lots of adults have ruined lives with their trips."

"It just makes me angry, knowing other people are out there making changes to my life that I don't even know about. Other people shouldn't be allowed to interfere that way. Someone should try to stop it." I felt the heat rising to my ears.

"People have. But lobbyists are powerful. And there's never been a persuasive enough reason to put an end to it. Even death hasn't been enough of a deterrent." She shrugged her shoulders in defeat. "If death hasn't convinced lawmakers, I don't think there's anything that will bring an end to time travel."

I pulled at the frayed end of the hoodie string, deciding whether to go on.

"If the death of a person who's already living isn't enough, what about if time travel keeps someone from ever being born?"

"I don't think the government would see that as any different, do you?" she asked, taking another sip of her tea.

I shivered, either from the topic of our conversation or the temperature of the room. Mom noticed, pulling the blanket from the back of the sofa and tossing it over my legs.

"I don't know. Maybe," I said. "I think it would have to be. Because think about conception – if something changes at the moment life is created and DNA comes together in a different way than it did the first time, that's not just ending a life. That's playing God, don't you think?"

Mom slid across the couch and gathered me in her arms. "Oh, my sweet, idealistic Melody. You might think that, and I might think that, but lots of people might just think that's part of nature's selective process."

"It's not nature though. That's just the thing. It's us interfering with the way things ought to be!"

"What makes you so sure the alternate timeline isn't the way things ought to be?"

She was playing the devil's advocate. I'd learned over the years I could never discuss anything with my mother without her attempting to make me see both sides. It was one of the many negative side effects of being married to a senator for so many years, and although I understood where it came from, I definitely didn't like it. In fact, it drove me absolutely crazy.

"That's the stupidest thing I've ever heard," I countered. "The simple fact that it's an 'alternate' timeline means it isn't the intended timeline. Anything that's changed is wrong by default."

She made a sweeping motion with her arms around the room. "You're saying *this* is all wrong, based on the fact that both Brooke and Charlie changed their timelines?"

I bowed my head. Of course, she was right, but it seemed less dramatic since our lives found their way back to the original course despite the changes that were made. My changes could never be undone.

Vicki was never coming back.

"Where is all this coming from anyway? Did you see something in the news? Did something happen to somebody you know?"

I would never tell her about Vicki. She would hate me more than I already hated myself and I couldn't stand the thought of disappointing her. Not again.

"No. Just a class I took this semester. It got me thinking about the political process and how our laws are difficult to change. If there's one law I'd like to make, it would be one to abolish time travel. Too many lives have been destroyed already and who knows how many more will perish in the future." I thought about Vicki and the impact she may have made on the world. "We could lose the next Einstein and not even know it."

She ran her fingers through my hair, gently massaging my scalp. "If that's how you feel, then maybe you ought to try to do it."

I sighed. "I'm just one person, Mom. A single person doesn't create change like that. Especially against all those special interest groups. It's impossible."

"A single person is all it takes to create the kind of change you're talking about. You just need people who believe in and support you."

"I'm a child without a single supporter. And you said yourself lots of people are fine with the way things are. They certainly won't support me."

Mom sat up, pushing me off her lap and turned me by the shoulders so we were facing one another.

"Melody Johnson, I support you. I always have and I always will. And your brother supports you. Brooke does too. And I think there's a certain football player who would have your back even if you tried to make beer and nachos illegal. So don't say you don't have a single supporter. And now that I think of it, I bet there's someone else I know who might be willing to help with your cause, assuming you're serious and this isn't just some whim."

It wasn't a whim. I'd never felt so passionate about anything in my entire life.

"Who?" I asked.

"Senator Turner, of course. Where do you think she stands on time travel?"

I had no idea. It was never something we'd discussed. At least I didn't think it was, but there was no way of knowing for sure given my missing months.

"You should give her a call," Mom continued when I didn't respond. "Let her tell you you're crazy. She just might." She kissed me on the forehead. "Or maybe she'll become your biggest supporter."

Chapter Twenty-Five

Christmas was bittersweet. For the first time in my life I spent the day away from Mom and Charlie and celebrated instead with Nate's outrageous family. The sheer number of Johansens all under one roof ensured there was never a quiet moment, and I soaked up all the commotion as a means of distracting me from what I was missing at home.

When he suggested I spend the holiday at his house I initially balked. Although I was tempted by the idea of waiting together in our pajamas for Santa on Christmas Eve, sipping hot cocoa in front of a crackling fire, I hated the thought of not being home. What finally made my decision was realizing it would be Mikey, not Vicki, who would be celebrating his first Christmas. Having to spend the day with him would only depress me further, and I knew I would have difficulty maintaining a cheerful façade, considering my composure was being held together with string and paperclips.

When I arrived at Nate's on Christmas Eve, he launched immediately into a prepared pep-talk as he helped carry my gifts for his family into the house.

"You're about to embark upon your first Johansen Christmas," he laughed, taking an especially large package from under my arm. "I just want to warn you that it might be a bumpy ride. And remember, whatever they tell you about me is probably a lie."

I set down my bags on the driveway's thin coating of snow so my hands were free to brush the disheveled mess of hair off his forehead. There was no denying how lucky we were to have been given a second chance. I knew if it hadn't been for my trip, his family's Christmas would have been marred by his addiction and I would have been miles away instead of nestled in his arms.

I also knew Vicki would have still been alive.

A lump formed in my throat but I was resolved to keep my sadness at bay. I refused to let my emotional instability ruin the day.

"Your family is crazy," I said finally. "And I think you fit right in."

He kissed me tenderly on the lips. "I think you fit right in too."

We spent Christmas day watching his thirteen nieces and nephews tear through scores of presents, each one more exciting than the last. It was fun to experience the holiday through the children's eyes even though, as Nate predicted, it was indeed a bumpy ride, with squabbles between his siblings throughout the day. Despite it all, the most pleasant surprise was the acceptance I was shown by his family. Not only was I given a place of honor at the family table, but I was also showered with handmade gifts and heartfelt compliments.

"You're the best thing that's ever happened to my boy," his mother said as we wrapped leftovers at the kitchen table together while his sisters washed the dishes. "I've never seen him so happy or so focused. If he'd gotten grades like this in high school, maybe he'd have gone to Stanford or Harvard!"

"Well, he wouldn't have met me at Stanford or Harvard," I laughed. "I had a bit of trouble in high school myself."

"It's no matter," she said, folding a drumstick into a sheet of aluminum foil. "With his performance at UVA, I'm sure by this time next year we'll be hearing from potential agents about the upcoming draft for sure. No way the NFL will pass over his talent."

I wanted to say something to her on Nate's behalf. Explain that he didn't want the life of a professional athlete. But I knew it wasn't my place. That was Nate's battle to fight, not mine.

And since I'd decided to formally approach Senator Turner about writing a bill to end time travel, I knew in the months ahead I'd have my own uphill battle to face.

During the week between Christmas and New Year's, while Nate defeated zombies and assassinated virtual drug lords on the refurbished game console from his brothers, I sat beside him on the couch scouring the internet for cases and laws that could set precedents for my bill. I quickly learned I was not the first to bring the cause before Congress, and that obviously, since time travel remained sanctioned by the government, every attempt to end it had been unsuccessful. The brightest spot in my research was discovering Senator Turner's stance on time travel; that she had voted against any bill that eased restrictions throughout her career.

"Whatcha working on over there?" Nate asked, tossing a controller in my direction.

"Just some research," I said evasively, having decided not to share my plan with him until after I had an opportunity to speak with Turner. "Probably nothing you'd be interested in."

He stood up and stretched, stiff from too many hours in front of the TV. "You've been at it for three days straight," he grumbled. "I was hoping today we could get out and do something fun, but I guess we don't have to if you'd rather hang out with your tablet instead of me."

It wasn't like Nate to complain and I knew he was only upset because I wasn't making the best use of our time together. How quickly I'd forgotten how awful life had been without him. I turned off my tablet, set it aside and dedicated the rest of my vacation to fostering our second chance. We spent the remainder of the week sledding with his nephews, baking cookies with his mother, and hanging out with a bunch of his old high school friends.

It was blissful in its normalcy.

However, as soon as I returned home after New Year's, I wasted no time refocusing on my agenda by contacting Senator Turner on her personal line. I knew it was bold to call her without going through the proper channels, but she'd given me the number in good faith to use if I should ever need her assistance, and with two solid weeks of research under my belt, I was ready to discuss my plan to abolish time travel.

"Melody! It's so nice to hear from you! Happy New Year!" she said when she realized who was on the phone. "How was your fall semester?"

"Happy New Year to you too," I replied. "School was great, thank you."

"I'm glad to hear it! You know, I was looking over our staff list for this summer and am so glad to see you'll be joining us again. You're such a delight to have around. Is that what you're calling about, because I can assure you your application was accepted."

I didn't want to sound ungrateful, but my summer internship was literally the last thing on my mind. "I'm so glad to hear I've been chosen and I appreciate the opportunity, but if you have a minute, there's something else I was interested in speaking to you about."

"Oh! Do you need something for a class assignment? I'm sure one of my aides would be happy to help you out."

"Actually, no. I was wondering if you think it might be possible to put an end to government sanctioned time travel? If so, I'd like to propose a bill."

I closed my eyes while I waited for her to respond, listening to her shallow breathing on the other end of the line. It was clear I'd startled her with my request.

"Well my goodness, that's a noble pursuit, but I'm not sure you're aware of the time and dedication an undertaking of this magnitude would require. I'm honored that you've come to me about it, but you must know that you're not the first person who has attempted to pass a bill through Congress against time travel. It's a pretty solid institution at this point."

I felt my chances slipping through my fingers in the same way Vicki disappeared from my life. I couldn't risk letting the opportunity pass me by, and so when I opened my mouth to speak, it was as if I was releasing the floodgates of a rain swollen river.

"Senator, something tragic has happened in my life, and I believe I have an angle to approach the removal of government funding for time travel which hasn't been addressed before. I would write the entire bill myself, do all the research, all the legwork, and I certainly wouldn't expect you to spend any time on this unnecessarily. All I need is for you to sponsor and introduce it. That's it. Truly, it would mean the world to me."

She was silent. I imagined her drumming her fingers on her desk as she often did when she was thinking.

"A new angle, huh? Are you sure about that?"

I forced myself to breathe. She was actually considering it.

"Yes, ma'am. I've read every bill to abolish government sanctioned time travel from the last thirty years and I am sure what I am proposing has never been discussed."

"Oh really?"

"Yes, ma'am. I found an old rider bill that was passed back in the 1990's. It's still on the books and I believe I could use it as a basis for the elimination of government-funded time travel."

"On what basis?"

I hesitated. I knew if I was going to go through with my plan I was going to have to tell her the truth about my own time travel experience and all that it entailed. But it wasn't something I was ready to discuss quite yet.

"On the basis of something I'm not comfortable talking about over the phone."

She chuckled heartily. "I knew I liked you, girl!" she laughed. "A rebel after my own heart!" I could hear her rustling papers on her desk. "Well, listen. You've got me. I'm intrigued. But I'm stuck here in DC for the rest of the month. Can you come by my office one day next week and bring everything you've got?"

I jumped out of my chair. "Yes, ma'am!"

"Well, okay then!" I could hear her smiling. "Let me transfer you to my administrative assistant and she'll let you know when I'm available. Sound good?"

"Sounds great," I told her. "See you next week."

Chapter Twenty-Six

I spent the next six days collecting my thoughts and research to present to Senator Turner.

"I'm heading into DC to meet with her about my proposed bill tomorrow," I told my mom over cornflakes.

"Want me to come along?" she offered, pouring herself a second cup of coffee and joining me at the table.

Knowing I might need to tell the Senator about my trip, the last thing I wanted was my mom tagging along. Having her with me would prevent me from being candid in our discussion.

"Nah," I said. "The meeting is something I need to do alone. But thanks for having my back."

As it turned out, I didn't have to worry very long about piquing the senator's interest as she was thoroughly intrigued by the research I presented over dinner at the 1789 Restaurant.

"Tell me more about this bill," she said, taking a small bite of her beet salad.

"Well, back in 1995 Congress passed something called the Dickey Amendment which was an appropriation bill rider attached to The Balanced Budget Downpayment Act. At that time the government had been through a series of furloughs and the rider sort of snuck through on the heels of the budget act. I don't think it even came to a vote on the house floor if you can believe that."

"I can believe it, but I don't understand how this amendment has anything to do with time travel. It hadn't even been discovered at that point."

I nibbled on a slice of Gouda from my cheese plate and prepared for the potential serious ramifications of what we were about to discuss. I hoped Senator Turner was as trustworthy as she appeared.

"The amendment itself doesn't have anything to do with time travel. It has to do with stem cell research."

She set down her fork and narrowed her eyes. "This sounds like dangerous territory, Melody."

I wiped my palms on the linen napkin in my lap. I couldn't stop sweating.

"Senator, there's something I need to confess, however by doing so I might be implicating myself in a crime. If this isn't something you're comfortable hearing, I completely understand. But to fully understand how my research relates to abolishing time travel, I think it's necessary for me to be honest with you. If you are unable to keep my secret for any reason, please just let me know and we can end our conversation now."

Her eyes widened. "My goodness, Melody. What have you gotten yourself into?"

"It involves the use of my trip, ma'am. I don't want to get you into any trouble by telling you my secret, and I don't know if you're bound to report crimes..."

"Whatever you tell me will remain between the two of us," she interrupted. "We can decide together if there's something we need to share with other people."

I hoped what she was saying was true. "You won't get in trouble for not reporting my confession?"

"We can forget this conversation ever happened if that's what you choose," she said, pretending to zip her lips.

"And you're not going to turn me in?"

She smiled warmly. "You're the best intern on my staff. I couldn't stand to lose you."

My mouth was thick and parched. I took a sip of spring water from the oversized goblet beside my plate and convinced myself for the hundredth time I was doing the right thing. I knew Vicki wasn't the only child whose life was erased from history because of time travel, but if I had anything to say about it, she would be one of the last.

"I used my trip in the fall," I began. "I went back to August of my first year and only stayed for twenty-four hours. When I returned from my trip I discovered something terrible happened simply because I travelled."

"Are you sure it was because of your trip? The authorities obviously weren't alerted since you were never detained."

I nodded. "I'm sure of it. The timing's too perfect. I had no idea taking my trip was going to result in my niece no longer being with us, but that's exactly what happened."

What remained of the senator's salad lay long-forgotten on her plate. "If you killed her, you would have been arrested. You must be mistaken about the cause."

I knew from Brooke's experience that changes resulting in death weren't always discovered, but I didn't believe it was a lack of monitoring which had prevented my arrest. I simply assumed that details of conception were never taken into consideration.

"I didn't realize the date of my trip was also the date of my niece's conception. By slightly altering the timeline on the night she was created, I prevented her from being conceived. When I returned, a different baby had been born in her place. I know this single event cannot be the only instance of this occurring. Because of time travel, my niece Vicki was replaced by someone else. Her creation was prevented because her embryo was altered by time travel."

Turner chewed nervously at her thumbnail. "And how does the Dickey Amendment relate to these events?" she breathed.

I composed myself, surprised by how fiercely the retelling of events unnerved me. "The amendment bans federal funding for all research involving the creation or destruction of human embryos. It also bans funding if the embryo is subjected to injury or death. I figure if there's already a law in place banning the government from funding an activity which destroys embryos, that sets a pretty strong precedent for banning funding of time travel, especially considering its potential to do the same thing."

"I see." Turner was quiet for a moment, digesting the implications of my findings. "When you returned, you said a different baby had been born. The embryo wasn't destroyed so much as changed."

I hadn't considered that reality. "I suppose so," I said. "I knew Vicki though, in the original timeline. And now she no longer exists. I have a nephew instead. Vicki's genetic material was replaced by someone else's."

The senator picked up her fork and pushed her salad greens distractedly around her plate. "I believe without a doubt that you have uncovered the most viable argument against time travel I've ever heard. But if we present this with the hope of banning all funding, there can be no holes. No chinks in the armor. We would need other cases, especially ones in which viable embryos weren't just replaced but actually ceased to exist because of time travel."

"Can we do that?"

"I have a few connections within the Time Travel Administration. I might be able to pull a few strings and call in some favors. There are records kept for every trip, it's just a matter of gaining access to them."

"And what about my trip?" I thought about the blatant changes I'd made to the timeline and the afternoon I spent with Nate. I knew if I came under scrutiny there was a chance I could go to jail.

She took a sip of her chardonnay. "You're worried about them detaining you for this? There's no way an arrest would be justified. That's the whole reason this argument is a legitimate stance against the continued use of time travel. You had absolutely no control over how that embryo reformed. The mere act of traveling placed your niece's life in jeopardy, and you cannot be held personally responsible since there is no way to predict how DNA will combine in any given case. Time travel alone is the only thing to blame for keeping her life from beginning."

I tucked my chin and folded my napkin in my hands. If felt good to hear the words spoken aloud, pardoning me for my transgressions. I didn't know if I would ever be able to fully forgive myself for Vicki's loss but being exonerated by someone else was a start. Even still, I knew the true motivation for the use of my trip was forbidden, leaving me too ashamed to look Turner in the eye. I needed to tell her the truth of why I feared incarceration.

"The embryo wasn't the only change that occurred as a result of my trip."

She scoffed. "Melody, trust me, you're not the first person to cause changes during a trip."

I peered up at her from beneath my hair, obscuring my face.

"I did it on purpose though."

She was grinning at me. "Doesn't everyone?" she laughed. "Honey, your secret's safe. I promise. And we can make sure to keep all of our findings confidential, including yours. No one is going to jail for this. I promise."

Before sharing our heartfelt goodbyes, Turner agreed to reach out to her connections at the TTA so we could begin investigating other possible cases of embryonic destruction caused by time travel. Meanwhile, I was responsible for drafting the bill as quickly as possible, knowing the longer it took, the less likely the bill would be seen by the sitting Congress. She explained that in addition to the actual drafting, we would also need time to consult with an attorney to assist us in rewriting the proposal into legislative language. When it was finished, Turner would need to circulate the bill to other congressmen in the hopes of gaining co-sponsors to demonstrate a base of support before formally submitting it to the clerks of the senate floor.

There was a lot of work to do and not enough hours in the day to do it, but I knew I could only live with myself knowing I'd done everything possible to assure what happened to Vicki would end up serving the greater good.

I drove back home confident in my ability to make big changes in the world. I only wondered if the pride of success would ever be enough to ease the pain of losing Vicki.

Part Three

Spring Semester — Third Year

Chapter Twenty-Seven

I nodded off in my women's studies lecture for the third time, roused only by the chaos of the class's dismissal. I was pushing myself too hard — between a full class schedule, homework assignments and commitments to friends, there was no time during the day to draft my bill. I spent most nights holed up in a private study room in the basement of the library poring over files passed to me by Turner's connection, Jeff Armstrong, at the TTA. Slowly, over the course of several weeks, the outline of my bill was beginning to take shape, but unfortunately my narrow focus had already begun to affect the other facets of my life.

"We're all going to The Corner tonight, Mel. Are you coming with us?" Lesley asked as we walked from the parking lot to Nate's apartment.

I was drained and the thought of spending the night in a loud, stuffy bar was anything but appealing.

"I don't think so," I told her. "I've got some homework to catch up on."

She rolled her eyes and pulled her snow cap over her ears. "Nate's gonna kill you. You haven't been out with us at all since we got back from winter break. What's going on with you?"

I shrugged nonchalantly but knew her analysis was astute. I'd gone into hyper mode, channeling my energy into drafting the bill at the expense of everything else. It was a familiar ritual, one that had played out many times before in my life. My father's death and my relationship with Nate were the only two catalysts which had swayed me from my focus in the past. I wondered if anything short of the bill's passing would slow me down this time.

"I just have a tough set of classes this semester, that's all, and I'd appreciate if you didn't give me a hard time about it, thank you very much."

"Whoa! Touchy! Okay. I'll back off. But I can guarantee Nate won't give you the same leniency. I heard him telling Tyree the other day how much he misses having you around. He didn't say it in so many words, but Tyree teased the crap out of him about it anyway. You don't watch it, you might just lose him."

I didn't know what made me angrier – Lesley thinking Nate would break up with me over not going out to a bar or me admitting she was right. I threw my hands in the air.

"Fine! I'll go to The Corner tonight if it will make everyone happy!"

"Whatever," she said as we reached the front porch. "Spending time with us should make you happy but it doesn't feel much like it lately."

She opened the door and without another word I followed her inside. Nate and Josh were stretched out on the threadbare, thrift store couch playing video games while Tyree made himself a sandwich in the kitchen.

"Ladies," Josh greeted us without looking up from the television.

"Dudes," Lesley replied, collapsing on the cushion beside him.

"Hey, stranger," Nate nodded, glancing up from the game to smile at me. "Long time, no see. Where ya been hiding?"

"I've been around. Here and there," I said, tossing my bag on to the nonfunctioning recliner beside the sofa before settling myself on the floor between his knees.

"You gonna grace us with your presence at Chase's birthday celebration tonight?" he asked.

I could feel Lesley glaring into the back of my head.

"Yes." I relented. "I'll be there. Wouldn't miss it for the world."

"Don't sound so enthusiastic," Tyree called from the kitchen. "It's like we're dragging you to a seminar on tooth decay."

"Or scoliosis," Josh chimed in.

Before I could respond to their sarcasm, my phone began vibrating in my pocket. A check of the screen confirmed the call was from Jeff, my connection at the TTA.

"I've gotta take this," I said, excusing myself to Nate's bedroom. I closed the door behind me before answering the call.

"Hello?" I said.

"Hello, Melody? It's Jeff. Do you have a minute?"

"Yeah. Of course. Please tell me you found something."

He chuckled into the receiver. "Yeah. I actually found more than one something. I found six somethings."

A wave of relief washed over me. Jeff had spent over a month searching unsuccessfully through the travel log database for evidence of other babies who no longer existed because their original timelines were altered by time travel. I hoped he'd found the break we were looking for because without other cases to support the cause, I would be forced to expose my own experience.

"Six!" I cried. "Jeff that's wonderful news! Were they all viable embryos that were born in their original timelines?"

"Yes. And none of those children exist today. What's even better is two of them are exactly what we were hoping to find."

I held my breath. "Embryonic destruction?"

"Yeah. Full-term viable pregnancies the first time around. No baby at all when the traveler returned. A person and then nothing at all."

If I could have jumped through the phone to hug him I would have. Although I hated thinking of the children who were never born, it was thrilling to know there were other instances outside my own which could be used to demonstrate why it was illegal for the government to continue funding time travel. Even better was realizing I was no longer obligated to present my own case.

My only regret was that I couldn't share my excitement with Nate and the others.

"Is it safe to email the data to me?" I asked, electrified by the prospect of reading about the children firsthand.

"I can encrypt the files and send them from an undisclosed account. I'll keep searching for more, but I thought you'd want to know about these as soon as I found them."

"Yes, thanks so much, Jeff. I'll look out for the files and keep my fingers crossed you find more. Talk to you soon."

We ended the call and I couldn't stop myself from skipping around Nate's room. I was composing myself to return to the den when I turned around to find him glaring at me from the doorway. I couldn't imagine why he looked so hurt.

"Was that him on the phone?" he asked pointedly.

"Him who?"

He rolled his eyes in disgust. "Lesley told me about Jeff, Melody. She said you left your phone in her room last week, and she saw you had a bunch of missed calls from some Jeff guy. On top of that she says you haven't been coming home at night. She hears you sneaking into bed at three in the morning. Is Jeff the reason you've been too busy for me all of a sudden?"

I was taken aback. Nate thought I was seeing someone else. That I was sneaking off to be with Jeff instead of him in the middle of the night. I didn't know whether to be shocked or flattered, but I knew by the expression on his face that although I couldn't be completely truthful with him about who Jeff was, I needed to ease his fears about any possible indiscretions.

"That was Jeff on the phone, and he sort of is the reason, yes, but not in the way you're thinking. I promise you, there isn't anything bad going on," I told him calmly.

He shut the door and began pacing the length of the room, carefully avoiding eye contact with me. "You really expect me to believe, considering how 'tired' and 'busy' you've been recently, that there's nothing going on with some guy who's calling you all the time. It's awfully coincidental, Melody. I'm not an idiot."

For years I had lived under the assumption that Nate didn't have a single jealous bone in his body. It was kind of nice to know the thought of losing me to someone else bothered him more than a little. I perched myself at the foot of his bed and invited him to sit beside me.

"Please, Nate. Let me explain."

It wasn't necessary to share all the details of what I'd been discussing with Jeff or about the logistics of the bill, but I wanted to be as honest with him as I could. Lies only tore people apart.

Nate grunted as he sat beside me, his arms crossed defiantly over his chest. "I'm listening," he said.

"Okay," I began, reaching out to place my hand on his knee, "over winter break I met with Senator Turner about a new bill she's going to present to Congress later this year. I'm helping her draft the bill and Jeff Armstrong is one of her contacts who's been supplying me with the research information I need to write it. He has access to files I can't get to, so when he finds new information, I get a call. That's it. That's who he is and why he's been calling me. As for the late nights, I decided that instead of taking even more time away from you than I already have been to draft the bill, I would continue working on it overnight at the library so I wouldn't keep anyone else awake. I'm exhausted because I work all day on school assignments and work all night on the bill." I took his chin in my hand, forcing him to look at me. "I'm really sorry I let the whole thing get out of hand."

His expression softened. "This Jeff guy isn't a student?"

I brushed his bottom lip with my thumb. "Definitely not. I've never even met him. I think he's old, like in his fifties."

"You're not running off to be with him when you're not with me? You're not staying with him in the middle of the night?"

I laughed aloud. "No! Does that sound like something I would do? If you don't believe me you can talk to library security. Mr. Patterson will vouch for me."

"No," he admitted, bowing his head. "I believe you, and I don't need to talk to Mr. Patterson. Running around with some other guy doesn't sound at all like something you would do. But it does sound like you to take on more than you can handle and run yourself into the ground. It's just that you've forgotten all about having fun since we've been back. I miss having you around, Mel."

He was laying it on thick and his guilt trip was working. "I'm sorry. I miss being with you too. I just couldn't say no to this opportunity and I didn't know what else to do." I hated seeing him so sad. "I'll scale back. I'll tell her I can't commit as much time to it," I blurted out.

He lifted his face and I couldn't gauge his expression. "That's stupid, Mel," he said. "This is what you want to do with your life. You should write the bill." He paused, placing his hand on my thigh which sent a burst of electricity through my body. "I'm glad you're not cheating on me."

I crawled into his lap, straddling his torso, and was overwhelmed by the memory of losing him to his addiction. I brought my lips to his, kissing him with a fierceness that caused him to initially recoil. He quickly reconsidered, wrapping me in his loving embrace - a fervent reminder of just how glorious it felt to be alive.

"You have no idea the lengths I would go to in order to preserve this relationship," I said after he placed a final kiss tenderly on my forehead. "I would never do anything to jeopardize what we have. Ever. If that means cooling it on the bill, I cool it on the bill."

He shrugged. "You don't have to do that. We'll figure something out. At least now I know the truth. And I'm sorry I accused you. I should have just asked."

I tucked my head into the hollow of his chest. "There's no reason for you to apologize since I'm the one who should've just told you about the project from the beginning. I just wish Lesley had kept her nose out of our business though," I said, considering her betrayal. If only she had approached me first instead of going straight to Nate with her half-baked theories. "Now that I think about it, I'm actually pretty pissed," I told him.

"Don't be too hard on her. You know how she gets sometimes. Maybe she's tired of sharing and wants me to herself," he joked. "She saw this as an opportunity to get you out of the picture."

"That's not funny," I said. "She would never do that."

"You're right," he replied seriously. "Maybe she was just trying to be a good friend."

I scoffed. "To who? You or me?"

He shrugged. "You have to admit, it looked kind of bad from where she was standing. She probably just didn't want to have to be the one to confront you."

I considered our friends, waiting for us in the other room. They were probably wondering when the fireworks were going to start.

"I assume they all think I'm a horrible person?" I asked, motioning toward the door.

He unwound himself from under me and stood up from the bed, reaching out to take my hand.

"Nah. It's none of their business anyway. I'll let them all know it was just a big misunderstanding and leave it at that."

We celebrated Chase's twenty-first birthday together that night and for a little while I was able to focus on the people in my life who needed me to be present for them. By morning however, memories of the one tiny person who was no longer in my life called me to refocus on what could be done to assure her short life would count for something, and I snuck back to my bill writing before the sun broke the horizon.

Chapter Twenty-Eight

After Valentine's dinner at our favorite pizza place, Nate and I returned to my room for an MMA fight he was excited to watch on TV. As we sat together on my bed, I fingered the tiny amethyst hanging from a chain around my neck and rehearsed the speech I'd been planning in my head all week. My need to finish the bill was far too great, and as I continued to carve out time to work on it, Nate grew increasingly agitated with my inattentiveness. I knew it would do more harm than good to keep him in the dark about my motivation, and I had decided that perhaps it was time to involve him in the process. My only hope was that I would be able to convince him to help me without telling him about my trip or the changes I'd made to our timeline.

"Thank you again for the necklace," I said. "It's beautiful."

"I know how you like purple, so when I saw it, I had to get it. It's a perfect match for your ring." He took my hand and twisted the band of gold, a present from my grandmother that was still in my possession – having never been hocked by him to purchase pills.

My resolve wavered briefly but having him back in my life, clean and sober, only confirmed for me once again that my future was tied to his. We were destined to be together. And because I'd already committed to working with Senator Turner to end time travel, I knew I would never be successful without both his understanding and support with regard to my career aspirations. The only way to assure he wouldn't feel left out was to make him a part of the project.

I took a deep, cleansing breath and closed my eyes. "Nate, there's something I need to talk to you about."

He dropped my hand and backed away from me toward the foot of the bed, his eyes wide with feigned distress.

"Are you running away to join the circus?" he asked.

I groaned. It was just like him to make light of my attempts at a serious conversation.

"No. I'm not joining the circus."

"A convent then? Are you becoming a nun?"

"Oh my God, Nate, no! Can you just let me be serious for two seconds?"

My tone got his attention and he crawled back in my direction, laying his head in my lap. "Whatever it is, I'm all ears," he said, grinning up at me.

I looked into his eyes, and saw that below the silliness, there was an intensity conveying the depth of his commitment.

It made me want to share the truth. There was no turning back.

"I know how annoyed you've been with me recently and you've been completely justified in voicing your displeasure. I know I've been preoccupied writing this bill for Senator Turner."

"No kidding," he moaned. "We talked about this before. You were gonna tell Turner you had to cut back on the time you were spending on it. Guess you never told her, huh?"

I traced his earlobe with the tip of my finger. "That's just the thing. I couldn't really tell her I don't have the time because the bill wasn't actually her idea. It was mine."

"Yours? Is it for a class or something?"

"No. It's for real. When I approached her about it she offered to present it to Congress for me. I can't really back out, and the truth is, I don't really want to. But instead of sneaking away to work on it alone from here on out, I was kind of hoping you might be willing to be my assistant. It's an unpaid position, of course."

He looked bemused. "Okay, future Senator Johnson. I'll bite. What's this bill about that has you breaking every rule I ever taught you about taking time for fun?"

I couldn't lie to him. I needed him to understand so he would want to work beside me.

"I'm writing a bill to end time travel."

He laughed aloud and sat up, turning back to the MMA match. "That's a complete waste of your time, Mel. No one's going to pass that bill. Time travel is a huge deal for the government. It's an institution."

"It's unconstitutional," I snapped, disappointed he'd blown me off so easily.

"What's unconstitutional about it? Everyone gets their chance if they want it. I just can't believe you'd rather spin your wheels on a dead-end project like this than hang out with me." He shrugged. "It's fine though. Do whatever you want. Just don't expect me to waste the rest of my semester too. You're on your own I'm afraid."

As much as he didn't want to admit it, he was hurt. And as much as I didn't want to share with him the true reason behind my passion for the bill, I knew it might be the only way to make him understand that it wasn't a matter of me choosing something else over him. I had an obligation to fulfill.

Beyond convincing him to join me out of a selfish desire to spend time together, I also couldn't continue lying to him. My father had shown me just how destructive it was to build a relationship on a foundation of lies. I wouldn't make the same mistake with Nate.

"Do you remember during our first date when I told you about how my dad lied to my mom all those years about the fact that he was Charlie's biological father?"

"Yeah. Of course. Your family talks about it all the time." He turned his attention from the television. "It's not some sort of secret is it? Did I say something in front of them I shouldn't have?"

Nate was always ready to take responsibility and apologize for his behaviors, even if he wasn't at fault. It was one of the things I loved most about him but it was also the personality trait that led to his undoing when Sam had died.

"No. Not at all. It's just that his lies ended up causing a tidal wave of problems in my family, and we made a commitment to each other after everything came to light that we would never keep secrets from one another again." I paused, knowing I intended to keep a very big secret from Brooke and Charlie for as long as I was able. I continued, pushing the thought to the back of my mind. "I want it to be the same with us. I don't want us ever keeping secrets from one another."

Nate remained unfazed. "Sounds good. What do you want to know?"

I placed my hand on his chest. I could feel his heart beating steadily.

Mine was racing.

"It's not you who's keeping the secret. It's me."

He turned to me with a look that conveyed he'd been waiting for me to disappoint him.

"What is it, Melody?" he asked solemnly. "On top of all this bill business, what else do you need to tell me about?"

I was determined not to cry as I told him about taking my trip and the reason behind why I decided to travel back in time. I described everything that happened in the aftermath of Sam's death in the original timeline - the burden of his guilt, the addiction to hydrocodone, the lying, the stealing, and the end of our relationship.

He stood up and began pacing the room. I could feel his frustration as he tried to make sense of the bombshell I dropped on him.

"Why are you telling me all this? I became a junkie? I threw my life away so you swooped in as my hero and fixed everything? Is that it? Do you want me to thank you? Do you want some kind of award?" He stopped beside the bed, towering over me where I remained frozen. "And what the hell does this have to do with you wanting to stop time travel? It just doesn't make any sense! You got everything you wanted out of your trip but you don't think anyone else should have the same chance?"

He was furious now.

I'd hoped knowing the part he played in my decision to use my trip would spark his interest in joining me in my crusade against time travel. Unfortunately, it had the exact opposite effect. There was only one thing left I could think of which might possibly lure him to my side.

"I did get what I wanted, Nate. For you to have your future restored. And you'll never know how happy I am that you're back to your old self. But because I chose to use my trip, something happened I hadn't anticipated. Something amazing disappeared from my life when I returned."

He glared at me. "Which was what?"

Once I told him there would be no going back, but I was desperate for him to understand my point of view. I prayed Vicki would be the catalyst.

"Not a what. A who. Vicki was her name."

He threw his hands in the air. "Who the heck is Vicki?"

"Vicki was Brooke and Charlie's daughter. But she's not anymore because when I went back in time she wasn't conceived. Mikey was conceived instead."

He lowered his chin, raking his fingers through his hair.

"You went back in time to save me and your niece disappeared?"

I stood up and attempted to fold myself into his arms but he withdrew, backing deliberately away from me.

I grabbed for his arm. "Yes, but I don't blame you, Nate…"

"You went back in time to save me and when you came back your niece was gone?!" he said again, glaring at me from just out of reach. "Are you kidding me? What the heck is wrong with you? What kind of person would tell someone something like that? Like it's my fault or something!"

I should have seen his reaction coming.

"No, Nate! Not at all!" I cried. "This isn't about you. It's about me wanting to make sure that no other embryos are ever destroyed by time travel. The only way to do that is to cut off government funding. Please, I want you by my side! I need your support!"

He backed away from me, shaking his head in disbelief.

"This is too much to handle, Melody," he said at last, snatching his coat off the floor. "It's like I don't even know who you are anymore. You go and use your trip to fix MY life, and when you realize you've messed up something in YOUR life, you sneak around and lie to me about what you're doing and why?"

"I'm still the same!" I pleaded. "Please don't go. I'm so sorry I upset you with all of this. I was just trying to help you understand."

"Oh, I understand," he spat at me as he reached the door. "I understand you're a control freak who can't just leave well-enough alone! I can't do this with you right now. In fact, I don't think I can do this with you ever."

Without so much as a glance over his shoulder, he slammed the door behind him, and I was left with a heart full of regrets.

Chapter Twenty Nine

I waited all evening for him to return. I thought for sure he would creep into my room in the middle of the night, steal under the covers and admit to the righteousness of my actions. I didn't need an apology, only his understanding.

As it turned out, I didn't get a single expression of regret or support, and morning found me alone. As I poured myself a bowl of cold cereal, it became obvious that my plan had backfired. Instead of seeing the value in the work I was doing, Nate focused solely on his role in what he saw as my endless string of mistakes.

I went about the day as I did every other. I attended my classes. Completed my assignments. Continued drafting my bill. The only difference was instead of scheduling a few stolen moments with Nate, I systematically avoided all the places I knew he would be. I wanted to give him the time and space he needed to come to terms with the knowledge and repercussions of my trip.

And so, I waited in the hope that he would eventually return.

As the hours became days and the days became weeks, my patience began to wear thin. Anxiety played at the fringes of my focus and Nate's personal well-being gave me pause. His proclivity for blaming himself about things that were out of his control made me wonder if his reluctant return stemmed from a sense of culpability surrounding Vicki's death. It would be just like him to personalize the tragedy.

Under the guise of a concerned girlfriend, I approached two of his professors about his conduct and was assured there had been no change in his attendance or academic performance. It was reassuring to know he wasn't exhibiting signs of any addictive behaviors but that knowledge did little to ease my growing apprehension surrounding our estrangement.

For her part, Lesley remained fairly neutral. Although she still saw Nate and the others socially, she refused to convey accounts in either direction. I deduced from our passing conversations that she was in the dark about the true nature of the rift between us. Instead she continued to harbor reservations about my fidelity. I tried not to let her distrust bother me, but it was obvious to both of us that what was left of our friendship was suffering because of it.

In light of the social instability in my life, I did the only thing I knew how to do which was to throw myself into my work. It was a terrible coping mechanism, but sadly, it was all that I had, and in the darkest hours of the morning it gave me something to think about beside the many ways my instincts were forever navigating me in the wrong direction. I'd been so sure Nate was destined to be a permanent fixture in my life that I'd forced the outcome, bending fate to my own will by using my trip. By mid-March I'd convinced myself that our break-up was just Fate's way of reestablishing the destiny that was already determined for the two of us. If we were never meant to stay together, it was something I could live with, but knowing time travel had the capacity to prevent people from ever being born was not.

Senator Turner, Jeff Armstrong, and I met for a full day at her home during spring break to discuss the next step with regard to the bill. I presented them with my finished draft, which after several thorough readings, she happily approved.

"You're a gifted writer, Melody," she said, handing the document across the table to Jeff. "Your ideas are well thought out and are presented in a way that's easy to understand. All that's left is to forward this on to my team of attorneys. I must tell you though, regrettably, once they muck it up with their legal jargon, I'm afraid it won't be quite so easy to comprehend. For that reason, I hope you don't mind if I submit your version for peer review to drum up some bi-partisan support."

My heart swelled with joy. "Do you really think we have a chance to end funding with this?" I asked.

She nudged Jeff who was reading through the document. "You're on the inside. What do you think?"

He lifted his eyes from the paper and lowered his glasses to the tip of his nose so he could see us clearly.

"I didn't imagine when I agreed to help you that I could be putting myself out of a job, but I gotta tell you ladies, this case is air tight. Technically, I don't know why this wouldn't pass..." He pulled at his greying moustache.

"But?" I asked, sensing there was more he wanted to say.

He flipped back to the front page of the document.

"But you can't account for people's emotions. There are those who feel the ability to time travel is a right, not a privilege. And typically, people don't like having their rights challenged."

"The right of one citizen to time travel doesn't override the right of another to exist," I explained.

He pushed his glasses back onto the bridge of his nose and began rifling through his own stack of papers.

"I agree wholeheartedly with you, but I'm a realist. I know what you're going to be up against and I just worry that your skin's a little thin. The cold, hard world of politics might not be the place for a girl with a heart like yours," he said smiling. "Now about those additional cases I found..."

He handed me a manila envelope, and I wasted no time spilling the contents onto the table. There were three pages of names, all belonging to people who existed before time travel disrupted their conception.

"How many are there?" I asked.

"By my last count, two hundred-seventeen since the government began regulating time travel," Jeff replied. "And fifty-three of those embryos were destroyed altogether. For what it's worth, I'd say you have yourself a pretty strong case."

"I'd say so," Senator Turner agreed, helping herself to one of the sheets. "The challenge is going to be keeping all of these cases anonymous, as well as your involvement, Jeff."

He rocked on the two back legs of his chair. "You don't have to worry about me, ma'am. I got a job at the TTA thirty years ago because I wanted to be close to the enemy, so to speak. If this bill's successful and the government defunds the program, I'll just go on and retire. I'll be just fine. And if by some chance my name leaks with regard to this investigation, I'll own it proudly. It's been an honor to serve you two ladies."

Turner placed her hand on top of Jeff's. "Without your documentation to support the theory behind the bill, we wouldn't stand a chance. Thanks for all your help."

Turner returned to Washington with my bill which she began circulating to her colleagues in an effort to gain support for our cause.

I returned to school and existed.

My course load kept me occupied for a majority of the time, providing a modicum of distraction from my inner turmoil. I could make it from breakfast to lunch without thinking of Vicki or Nate at all, and then I would spot him across the quad with the guys, laughing together as if he hadn't missed a beat in my absence. It was all I could do not to call out or race to join him. I tried desperately to focus on the positive - that he was at school, thriving because of me instead of wasting away at home or in jail. Knowing his life was better because of the decision I made, regardless of whether we were still together, helped ease the sadness.

Until the moment it would overtake me in the middle of the night, leaving me staring at the walls, my head swimming with regret.

If only...

If only…

If only I would have just kept my mouth shut instead of being so righteous.

My subconscious tormented me during the nights of waiting for the elusive moment when things would finally Get Better. Visions of two children beset my dreams. One was pleasant and demure, with a head of chestnut curls; the other clever and rambunctious, with a golden mop atop his head. Each time they visited was the same. The scene always began with the little girl sitting quietly along a riverbank, dipping her toes into the water which trickled along the rock bed. The water was cool but not cold, and I allowed the serenity of the moment to wash over me. There was peace.

But then, just as her presence began soothing my soul, he would arrive, stomping through the shallows like an animal recently released from his cage. He called our names, crying out for us to join him in his revelry. When we didn't accommodate his wishes, he splashed our faces, delighting in our pleas for him to stop. This continued, until enraged by our defiance, he would approach the girl and devour her bite by bite, leaving no trace of her behind.

The dreams grew increasingly vivid as Easter approached, and I knew I needed to come to terms with Mikey's presence in my life before going home to face him over the holiday. It was irrational to harbor resentment toward a child who was blameless with regard to Vicki's absence, but the longing in my heart could not be squelched.

Chapter Thirty

My family was waiting for me Friday night when I arrived. Mom was curled up on the couch, engrossed in her favorite reality television show, while Brooke and Charlie occupied Mikey on the floor.

"Hey, Mel," Charlie said, standing to greet me with a hug. "Feels like I haven't seen you in a year."

I felt the same way and although I'd been busy, I regretted not finding time to get home at least a weekend or two since winter break. The truth was I'd been avoiding them because of Mikey, but was resolved to make peace with my nephew and find solace in my family's unconditional love.

"I've missed you guys," I replied, relishing the warmth of his embrace. "It's good to be home, even if it's only for a couple days."

"We've been telling Mikey all about you, haven't we buddy?" Brooke cooed at the baby crawling in my direction. "We've been showing him your picture and teaching him your name. That's Aunt Melody, Mikey. Go give her kisses."

I stooped down as he approached cautiously, stopping several times to look back at his mother for approval. He was twice as big as I remembered and I felt a twinge of regret for missing his first Christmas. His eyes were wide with anticipation and drool pooled under his bottom lip.

"It's okay," I said to him. "I came all the way home just for a slobbery kiss from you."

He stopped at my feet and I scooped him into my arms. He was sturdy and solid and despite my reservations, worthy of my love. Before I realized what he was doing, he planted his open mouth on my cheek and grunted, pleased with his performance.

"You're getting so big!" I said, tickling his tummy. "What are they feeding you to make you into a giant?"

He giggled wildly, a great belly-laugh of pure delight, and in that moment, I knew I could do it. I could love this baby not instead of Vicki, but in addition to. There was room in my heart for them both.

I sat on the floor and fed him from a package of bite-sized crackers Brooke dug from the depths of her diaper bag. I was impressed with how content he was to nibble his snack while I caught up with his parents.

"Mom told us all about the bill you're drafting with Senator Turner. We're so excited for your accomplishments and thrilled you would take on the cause," Charlie said, returning to his place beside Brooke on the floor.

With their openly vehement opposition to time travel, I knew they'd be interested in the bill's progress. The warmth of their pride began thawing the frozen ache of my regret.

"The bill is actually being rewritten by Turner's team of attorneys and I'm just waiting to hear back about whether she's garnered bipartisan support. The last time I talked to her she thought she might be able to formally introduce the bill on the Senate floor by the end of the month, as long as there were enough congressmen to support going forward."

Charlie shook his head, beaming at me from across the room. "I had no idea you had this fire inside of you, Mel. Every time I tried to talk to you about time travel after my disastrous trip, you blew me off. And I gotta be honest, with the way you used to talk when you were younger, I thought you'd take your trip no matter what. I just can't believe my little sister might be the one who could finally put an end to it. Where's all this passion coming from all of a sudden?"

I couldn't look him in the eye and focused instead on placing crackers into Mikey's plump little hands. I would never tell him about Vicki.

Ever.

"Like I told Mom, I took a class last semester and it just got me thinking about how dangerous traveling is in our society. Look how much trouble it caused in our little family. It made me really angry to think about all the things that have probably changed in my life as a result of other people's trips that I don't even know about. Not only that, but I hate knowing my future might change dramatically based on someone else's decision to travel. You wouldn't believe some of the stories I've read as part of our research. Just last week we came across a woman who used her trip when she was eighty-nine-years-old to go back in time to relive the early days of her marriage. When she returned after her trip, an entire side of her family tree was gone.

"Apparently, the son she conceived during the course of her trip in the original timeline was born a daughter instead, but unlike her son who married and had three children, the daughter never wed. Because her son was never conceived, his children were never born and neither were his eight grandchildren. They were all gone. Poof. And when you stop to consider how different the lives of the spouses must be now, since they were never able to marry their loved ones from the original timeline, it really makes your head spin. Knowing time travel is responsible for stuff like that going on in our world makes me angry. I just don't think it's right for the government to give people so much control of other people's lives through time travel, so I decided to try to find a way to end it."

Brooke stared at me as though she'd been punched in the gut. "Why wasn't the woman arrested? Her trip eliminated twelve people from the world. That's illegal."

I shrugged. "She didn't get arrested for the same reason you didn't get arrested over Mrs. Cooper. She wasn't in the monitoring demographic."

"But twelve people... surely someone must have noticed!"

219

I set Mikey on my lap and fed him another cracker. "That's just the thing. Until Jeff started snooping around in the files, no one knew but her. And besides, conception isn't a punishable offense. That's why it's the basis of my loophole."

Charlie couldn't contain his pride. "Most kids would have left a project as daunting as this one to the adults..."

I threw a cracker at his head. "I *am* an adult!"

"You know what I mean," he laughed, eating the cracker off the floor. "I'm just saying sometimes it's better if you don't know what you don't know. You're pretty naïve about the whole legislative process. You're getting ready to jump into a tank of sharks."

"And you think I'm going to get eaten alive?"

He looked to Brooke as if he needed rescuing.

"Maybe not now, especially considering you already found a precedent to end funding. How many hundreds of people before you overlooked that very law?" He crawled across the floor to scoop Mikey into his arms. "I just meant that most adults would have been so intimidated by the chips stacked against them, they never would have even gotten started. But not you. Your bill's on its way to Congress for crying out loud, Mel!"

"Your father would have been so proud," Mom gushed.

Charlie pretended to gag. "Our father would have ridden her coattails as long as the wind was blowing in the right direction while attempting to take credit for the bill at every opportunity. Not to mention that he'd resent the hell out of the fact he didn't think of it himself."

"Charlie," Mom scolded. "Enough."

He brushed her off and threw Mikey into the air above his chest, eliciting joyful squeals.

"He's in a good mood tonight," I commented, changing the topic. It was sweet to see Charlie playing with his son, roughhousing and tumbling around the floor. I never saw him carry on with Vicki that way.

"He's really turned a corner in the last couple months. It was rough going in the beginning, but he's really mellowed out." Brooke paused, watching her boys carry on. "Not that he still doesn't have his moments. Remember last week in the grocery store, Charlie?"

"Which time?" he laughed. "When he kept trying to pull cans of green beans off the endcap or the time he screamed bloody murder when we wouldn't let him hold that plastic duck?"

"That's right," she replied. "That stupid duck! I thought for sure someone was going to escort us out of the store with the way he was carrying on. You'd have thought we were breaking his legs!"

It was reassuring to know that even though I'd robbed them of their daughter, Brooke and Charlie seemed content with the result of the alternate timeline. Mikey wasn't Vicki, but he was their son, and they were happy in their state of ignorant bliss.

"Where's Nate?" Charlie asked, wiping the drool from Mikey's lips. "I thought for sure he'd be coming with you this weekend. Or is he doing the family thing at his house?"

I poured what was left of Mikey's crackers from the bag into my mouth and chewed slowly, giving me time to collect my thoughts. I figured they would ask about Nate eventually and was surprised they hadn't inquired about his absence earlier in the evening. Of course, I couldn't tell them why we had broken up.

But I also couldn't lie and tell them we were still together.

"He's not here because we broke up on Valentine's Day," I announced casually over my shoulder as I headed into the kitchen for a glass of water.

"You broke up?" Mom called after me. "Valentine's Day was over a month ago! What in the world happened, and why didn't you say something before now?"

I chugged an entire glass of water, filled the cup a second time, and returned to the family room to explain away our breakup as painlessly as I could.

"It's no big deal," I said finally, taking a seat beside Mom on the couch. "Nothing happened, per se. I just don't really have time to dedicate to a relationship right now, what with my course load and writing the bill and all."

"Seriously?" Charlie said. A knowing look passed between him and Brooke. "You two loved and supported each other through Sam's death and all the ups and downs of your relationship over the years and you broke up over not having enough time together?"

I was resolved to protect them from the truth, even if it meant throwing Nate under the bus.

"He didn't like that I was spending so much time working on the bill. It was a hard sell for him considering he doesn't support the theory behind it. I guess we had a difference of opinion and this particular difference was just too great to overcome," I explained with more composure than I felt.

"I'm sorry to hear that," Brooke said sincerely. "We all really liked Nate. He kept you... balanced."

What she really meant was that he kept me sane and prevented me from falling into old habits. Left to my own devices I continued to work myself into a stupor at the expense of everything else in my life. To that end, the bill couldn't pass quickly enough.

Luckily, I didn't have to wait long to hear back from Turner about our progress. She had garnered enough bipartisan support in both houses of Congress and planned to formally present the bill on the floor of the Senate the week after Easter.

Chapter Thirty-One

～◦◦◦◦◇◦◦◦～◦◦◦◇◦◦◦～

The attacks started immediately. Once the press got hold of Senator Turner's proposal, it spread like wildfire through the nation, fueling old rivalries and pitting coworkers, friends, and family members against one another. Like every politically charged campaign against time travel since its inception, protesters wearing the armor of scientific progress bubbled to the surface en masse. I'd underestimated the backlash of opposition from the scientific community as well as the emotional outcry from those who felt their right to travel was being placed in jeopardy.

I watched helplessly from school as the networks televised heated arguments from both sides of the debate. For her part, Turner worked tirelessly to gather support and present our findings. She shared the statistics of the lives lost through embryonic destruction as well as through punishable criminal offenses like the one for which Charlie had been arrested. She pleaded our case, stating that the Dickey Amendment set a strong precedent to ban federal funding for all instances where embryos were placed in harm's way or destroyed by any means. But after weeks of battling the other side, I knew our case wasn't going to be strong enough to end time travel. It was missing something that pie charts and grammatically correct speeches couldn't provide.

It was missing the human connection.

People were having trouble relating to our cause because there was no emotional attachment. No face to empathize alongside. No heart.

People didn't rally around computer generated bar graphs. They rallied around other people.

Our cause needed a champion.

A senate voting date was set for the first week of May, so I knew if we stood any chance of swaying opinions by winning the public's support, we needed to work quickly.

I placed a late-night call to Senator Turner's private line.

"We're losing, aren't we?" I inquired after Turner caught up briefly on my personal life.

"I wouldn't say we're losing, but the vote is split down typical lines. We need to influence quite a few delegates if we are going to win."

I didn't want to be the face of time travel abolition but perhaps I didn't have a choice. Perhaps it was my destiny.

I took a deep breath.

"I want to help," I said. "I think it's time for me to come to Washington."

"That's a sweet offer, Melody, but I don't know what you can do that isn't already being done."

I chewed at my cuticle. As soon as I spoke the words aloud I'd be committed to sharing my truth. It was now or never.

"I can tell everyone about my story. Get me a press junket. Let me do the morning news circuit. I think if people hear what happened to Vicki they might be more receptive to our cause."

There was silence on the other end of the line. She didn't speak for several moments.

"Ma'am?" I said.

She cleared her throat. "You told me from the beginning you wanted to remain anonymous to protect your family and to prevent your trip from coming under scrutiny. I don't think I can allow you to break your silence, especially when it might not be enough to make a difference."

"But it might be," I replied hastily. "And for Vicki's sake and the sake of all the other people who may never be born because of time travel, I'm willing to take that chance."

She was silent again. I imagined her rubbing her temples the way she did when she was stressed. Finally, she spoke.

"What if there might be another way to connect a story to our cause?"

"It needs to be a person. A face. Someone for people to relate to."

"Yes. I agree," she said. "But that person doesn't necessarily have to be you. Any chance you might be willing to fly out to Texas this weekend?"

I had no idea what she was proposing but it didn't matter. I was on board. "Of course. Yes. I'll do whatever I need to do to help."

"Great. I'll book you a ticket for tomorrow night and email you a file. I think there's someone you need to meet."

Less than twenty-four hours later I was in the air over Kentucky, halfway to Texas, munching on stale crackers and sipping from a two-ounce cup of soda. I'd read through Luciana's file half a dozen times and knew why she was the perfect champion for our cause. The only hurdle would be convincing her to share her story with the world.

A taxi delivered me to her house, a modest ranch on the outskirts of San Antonio. I had no idea what her emotional state would be, but I convinced myself that regardless of our meeting's outcome, I would leave her better than I found her. It took me several moments to work up the courage to knock on her door.

I was greeted by a petite Hispanic woman with soulful eyes and a cheerful smile.

"Can I help you?" she asked. A hint of her Latino heritage was still noticeable in her speech.

"Mrs. McArthur, my name is Melody Johnson and I was sent to speak with you by Senator JoAnne Turner because we need your help with something. I was wondering if you had a few minutes that I could speak with you about it."

After a slight hesitation she invited me inside and led me to an oversized sectional in the family room.

"Can I get you something to drink?" she asked.

"I'm fine. Thank you," I told her, taking a seat on the couch. There were photographs on the fireplace mantel of Luciana and her husband Jonathan at various vacation destinations as well as tchotchkes from their travels decorating shelves around the room. "You have a beautiful home," I said.

She chose a chair across from me, folding her legs beneath her as she sat.

"Thank you. I try to fill the space with memories. Most days it helps." She shifted her weight nervously as if she couldn't get comfortable. "You said there was something someone from the government needed my help with?"

I smiled genuinely at her, hoping to convey my intentions were pure. "I work for Senator Turner, and I don't know if you've been following the news at all, but she's proposed a bill to end government sanctioned time travel. It will be voted on next month."

I watched her face carefully for an indication of whether the bill would be something she'd be willing to support. Her eyes did not betray her emotions, so when she didn't speak, I continued.

"The bill itself was actually my idea, not Senator Turner's. I decided to work to defund time travel when, after taking my own trip, I returned to discover my niece had disappeared. As it turned out, I inadvertently traveled to the exact date of her conception and she was never created. My nephew Mikey was born in her place."

Tears pooled in the corner of Luciana's eyes. I didn't know whether to go on.

"Ay," she said at last, blotting the mascara from her lashes. "My niño too."

I leaned forward, sensing an opportunity to make a connection.

"Your son, Eduardo. The same thing happened to him?"

"Si," she replied. "No one told me it might happen."

I placed my hand on her knee, a gesture of solidarity. "Me neither," I said. "Would you mind sharing with me what happened, if it's not too difficult?"

She leaned back in the chair and closed her eyes. She was thinking about her little boy and I couldn't help but feel responsible for dredging up painful memories of her past.

"Jonathan and I had a beautiful wedding. It was small. Just a few family and friends. He was scheduled for deployment the following week, so we took only a four-day cruise to the Caribbean for our honeymoon to make sure we'd be back in time for him to ship out." She paused, turning to stare out the window so she wouldn't have to face me as she welled up for a second time. "I'd never been on a cruise before. It was wonderful. The most magical four days of my life."

She was crying in earnest now, and I handed her a napkin from my bag to wipe her cheeks.

"I remember calling him during his deployment to let him know he was going to be a dad. I'll never forget that day, when he told me he couldn't wait to raise our child together. The army let him come home for two weeks when Eduardo was born, and I thought then that saying goodbye when he left was the hardest thing I was ever going to have to do." She laughed feebly. "Little did I know."

She composed herself and I could tell she was mentally preparing to share the rest of her story.

"What made you decide to use your trip?" I asked.

"Jonathan came back from his deployment and was home for a little over a year." She glanced at a group of photos on the end table beside where I was sitting. "Before my trip, there was a picture of the two of them on a hike along the river. He carried Eduardo everywhere on his shoulders. They were really something together."

She shook her head. "Now I don't even have photos of my baby to help keep my memories alive."

She stopped speaking, seemingly lost in remembrance of her son, and I waited patiently for her to begin again.

"Just after the baby's second birthday, Jonathan got picked up for a stateside training rotation in Louisiana. The convoy was involved in an accident on the way and while most of the battalion walked away with only scratches, he and four other soldiers died from their injuries." She shook her head. "Two tours overseas and he ended up dying because one of his men fell asleep behind the wheel. What are the chances?"

"I'm so sorry, Mrs. McArthur," was all I could think to say. I hated making her upset.

"It happens, you know? When you're an Army wife the threat is always there. But then again, I guess the threat is always there regardless of what type of wife you are. Tragedies happen every day, don't they?"

"I suppose they do," I said, suddenly realizing the purpose of her trip. "And after he died, you went back to relive your honeymoon?" I asked.

She nodded. "It was the worst mistake of my life. If only I had known," she cried.

I knew it was unnecessary for her to finish telling her story. She had obviously reset her timeline during her trip and instead of conceiving Eduardo as she had the first time, she ended up never getting pregnant at all.

"I came back to nothing," she wept. "No husband, no child. I lost them both."

"I'm so very sorry for your loss," I said again as I moved to the floor to sit at her feet. "I can only begin to imagine your pain and grief, but your story is the reason I'm here. We are fighting to end time travel so other families won't be forced to live through losses like ours, but sadly we are losing that fight. People aren't connecting with our cause because we have no ambassador. No story for them to connect to." I placed my hand on top of hers. "I was hoping… *we* were hoping, that maybe you would be able to fill that role for us."

She peered down at me through her tear streaked lashes, disbelieving my request.

"You want me to tell them about Eduardo?"

"Yes. I need you to tell the world how time travel changed your life."

She pounded her fist into the arm of the chair. "It ruined my life!" she cried.

"I know. So please, Mrs. McArthur, say you'll help me pass this bill. I need you."

She didn't respond and I thought for a moment she was going to ask me to leave. And then she took my hand in hers.

Her voice was thick and her eyes blazed with the fervor of her grief. "I will help you. Just tell me what I need to do."

Chapter Thirty-Two

It took several days to arrange for Luciana's short-term relocation to DC. Turner set her up in a spacious downtown hotel room for use as home base while she prepped for her national debut. I met with her over the weekend she moved in, introducing her to Turner's staff and helping to acclimate her to the area. We briefed her on the bill's short history and rehearsed her speeches. By the time we were finished, I was confident our bill would pass.

And that's when all hell broke loose.

Turner booked Luciana's story exclusively to *Meet the Press*, but someone in their office leaked rumors of her account to the media the night before her interview was set to air. We woke Sunday morning to negative sound bites on every major network.

"They haven't even heard what she has to say and they're already trying to tear her down. They have no idea whether or not she's a 'religious zealot' or a 'fearmonger,'" I complained to Turner as we sat together in the green room waiting for Luciana's interview to begin.

Turner smiled broadly. "My sweet, innocent Melody, this type of publicity is a good thing, believe it or not. Our cause is finally gaining momentum and the opposition knows it. Up until this point they haven't felt threatened. The fact that they're stooping to straw man attacks means they're getting scared. Luciana is a slam dunk and they know it."

"You think so?" I asked hopefully.

She put her arm around my shoulders. "I know so," she said. "Let's just hope Luciana holds it together for this interview."

As it turned out, we had no reason to be worried about Luciana holding up under pressure. She sailed through the interview, relating her story of time travel destruction like a seasoned professional. Calls from each of the morning news programs came in before her segment cut to its first commercial break. We happily accepted all of the requests and after brunch together at Le Diplomate, Luciana and Turner boarded a plane for New York City. I, on the other hand, drove back to school alone to begin another week of classes, closing in on the end of my third year.

Lesley discovered me early Monday morning, still in my pajamas, glued to the television in the common room of our apartment.

"Is that the woman who lost her baby?" she asked, sitting beside me on the sofa.

I nodded.

"I heard about her on the radio yesterday," she continued. "Such a sad story."

I ignored her, focusing instead on Luciana's heartfelt proclamation in support of the bill.

"Do you think the bill will pass because of her?" she interrupted again.

I shrugged and tried not to be annoyed at Lesley for distracting me.

"This is your bill, right? The one to end time travel?"

As Luciana's segment ended, I turned to face Lesley, wondering how she knew about my involvement.

"He told us about it," she said, taking a sip of coffee from her mug.

"What did he say?" I asked her.

She swallowed her last mouthful of coffee and set her mug on the floor. "He said you needed time to yourself to do what you needed to do. He said the bill was important to you for some reason and that we should leave you alone." She picked up the remote and flipped to another morning news program. "So that's what we've all been doing."

I felt a strange sense of affinity toward him that he hadn't divulged all my secrets.

"That's all he said?" I asked.

"Yeah. Pretty much. None of us can figure out why ending time travel is such a big deal to you all of a sudden, but it seems like we shouldn't try to stand in your way when you have something in your life more important than we are."

I felt like I'd been slapped in the face.

"What's that supposed to mean?" I said, turning back to the television.

"I don't know. It's not always a bad thing I guess. You're just driven is all, in a way the rest of us aren't. Once you get going you don't know how to put on the brakes. Poor Nate just felt like he was some sort of road block I guess." She stood up and started toward her room. "But I'm happy for you that your bill's gonna pass. The only bad part is knowing I'll never get a chance to use *my* trip."

She disappeared into her bedroom and I stared blankly at the TV screen. I didn't know how to feel about my friends' perceptions of the bill or time travel or me for that matter. And although it was ridiculous to assume Nate hadn't told them anything about what I was working on, I wondered just how much he shared, especially considering Lesley's comment about not being able to use her trip. Did she judge me for having taken mine?

The worst realization to come out of our brief conversation was Nate's impression that my ambitions were more important to me than he was. I never thought of him as an obstacle but perhaps it was how he viewed himself. It broke my heart and I wondered how he would react if I approached him about it.

Alienating my friends was an unexpected side effect of my ambition and although my chosen path had obviously driven a wedge between us, I had come too far not to see the process through to the end. I just hoped when all was said and done there was still something left of our relationships to repair.

Before Lesley reemerged, Luciana appeared on her third news show of the morning. Poised and charismatic, she recounted her story to the audience, imploring viewers to let their respective congressmen know it was time to put an end to government sanctioned time travel.

"No mother should be forced to live without her baby," she wept into the camera.

Watching her raw emotion, I knew regardless of the outcome, I would be forever indebted to her. She brought a face to our cause with a humanity I could have never achieved. By serving as our willing ambassador, she protected me from revealing that I'd taken my trip and allowed Brooke and Charlie to live free from any grief the truth may have caused them. Putting an end to time travel was the only repayment I considered worthy of her tremendous effort.

I avoided news coverage for the rest of the day and instead wandered around school, alone with my thoughts. The day had grown warm and I shed my hoodie, wrapping it around my waist as I sat beneath the branches of a newly blossoming oak. The tree grew just outside the sports medicine hall where I assumed Nate was attending his weekly biomechanics class, and although I hadn't intentionally planned on ending up there, I wasn't averse to the possibility of seeing him.

While I waited for him to appear, birds chirped in the limbs above my head, ambivalent to my inner turmoil. How carefree to sing and soar above the clouds, unfettered by the emotions of a human heart.

Before the sun descended below the tree line, Nate emerged from the building, his backpack slung casually across his shoulder. Beside him was Erin Waters, a classmate, but also someone who I always viewed as a potential threat. Where I was serious, she was rambunctious. Where I was cautious, she was brazen. Erin was everything I wasn't and seeing the two of them together made me remember how different Nate and I truly were. I had known from the minute I met him that we were an unlikely pair. Perhaps it was better for him to end up with someone less driven and more open to his relaxed take on life.

They turned, heading away from me toward the parking lot and I stood up to leave, brushing the mulch from the back of my legs. My movement must have caught his attention because he turned to face me and our eyes locked. There was something in his reaction, the way his face softened, that caught me by surprise, and although I was expecting some show of anger, there was no indication that he still harbored any sort of resentment. I wanted desperately to go to him, but the moment I took a step forward, Erin grabbed his elbow, pulling him away. He turned from me and I wasted no time heading back across Grounds in the opposite direction.

I spent the evening by myself, holed up in my room watching the nation's reaction to Luciana's story. If I hadn't already been flustered by my encounter with Nate, watching the pro-travel zealots viciously attacking Luciana would have merely upset me. Unfortunately, confronting both blows in one day was more than enough to push me over the edge into full-blown 'eat a pint of ice cream by yourself' despondency.

As I sat listening to one commentator after another label her as a "progress Nazi" and a "scientific-rights opponent," I chalked up the day as just another low point in the tumultuous sea of my life. I'd lived through death, loss, and regret. What was one more day of sadness?

After listening to at least a dozen straw man attacks on Luciana and our message, I turned off the television and tried to sleep, but my brain kept replaying the vicious attacks on our cause.

"The proposed bill's goal is to take away your right to travel," one particularly outspoken congressman commented. "But if we start taking away every right that potentially affects other people, we won't have any rights left. People like Senator Turner and Mrs. McArthur would be happy if all of your rights were taken away."

I hoped Turner was correct in her assumption that the straw man attacks signaled a shift in the momentum – an indication that we were about to leave the opposition in our wake. If that was indeed the case, then I didn't understand why it seemed as though Luciana's story had set us back even further than it carried us forward.

It took several more hours to quiet my mind, and after effectively blocking the memory of Erin Waters walking with Nate, enjoying the benefits of a life I worked to restore, I finally fell asleep. I placated myself with the knowledge that I was working for the greater good, on Vicki's behalf, and that in the end, everything would work out as it should.

Chapter Thirty-Three

By morning, things were looking up. A handful of people with cases similar to Luciana's crawled out of the woodwork, proclaiming their support for the bill — among them, a couple from Arkansas who lost a daughter and an elderly man from Oregon who lost his grandson. Closer to home, I overheard a conversation at breakfast from a group of first-years at the table beside me defending the bill's position. Their enthusiasm shone as a glimmer of hope that not all was lost.

My phone vibrated just before lunch in the middle of my political theories class and when I saw who was calling, I slipped out the back door to answer.

"Melody, it's JoAnne. Any chance you could make it here to DC by tomorrow night?"

I tried to remember what day it was.

"Tomorrow's Thursday?" I said aloud, reviewing my schedule in my head. "I need to talk to a couple professors, but I should be able to make it," I told her. "Why? What's going on?"

"We're going to have a rally on the lawn in front of the Capitol at 5 PM. I don't think it's going to be too large of a gathering, but we got approval from the police department and I've invited the press, so hopefully it will drum up enough support to carry the bill through to legislation."

I knew at once the rally was something I needed to attend.

"I'll be there," I said.

"Great. I'll leave a press pass for you with one of my staff so you can come backstage if you want. Just stop by my office beforehand and I'll see you there." She paused, and I sensed there was something more she wanted to say. "I think the bill is going to pass, Melody. It's going to be my legacy to end time travel."

I considered her legacy and wondered about my own. What legacy was I to leave behind? No mention of my name would ever be linked in the history books to the defunding of time travel. Students would read about Senator JoAnne Turner and perhaps Luciana and Eduardo McArthur, but nowhere in the annals of history would there be a mention of Melody Johnson and her niece Victoria. We would be lost to time forever.

And I was surprisingly okay with that. I had no desire for fame and was content to sit back and let Turner take the credit for the law. It was enough to know I'd done what I could to prevent time travel from destroying other people's families.

I had no trouble getting permission to skip classes that day. When I told my professors I was planning to attend the Rally to End Time Travel in DC, they were happy to excuse my absence. One even offered extra credit if I wrote a short report about the event, which of course seemed ridiculous knowing the time and effort I'd already spent bringing the bill to fruition.

I arrived in DC on Thursday afternoon and spent over an hour walking the length of the mall by myself, absorbed by the beauty of the cherry blossoms blooming throughout the city. By the time I made it from Turner's office to the Air and Space Museum, I'd made peace with the reality of my situation.

Nate was happy. Brooke and Charlie were happy. Mikey was happy.

And regardless of whether or not my bill passed, things were going to be okay.

A stage was assembled in front of the Capitol at the far end of the mall and a crowd was beginning to form. Supporters from both sides of the debate appeared in droves with banners and signs declaring the legitimacy of one position over the other. A growing section of protesters stood beyond the police barricades, calling for an end to the diplomatic tyranny the bill represented to all Americans. I steered clear of the demonstrators and wove my way through the crowd to the staging area behind the platform.

"Melody!" Turner called to me from where she stood with Luciana. They were surrounded by her staff and several other supporters I recognized from TV, including the grandfather from Oregon.

I hurried to them, hugging Luciana tightly, grateful for the opportunity to share my appreciation for her dedication to our cause.

"I'm so sorry about the negative press," I told her after all the introductions were made. "I feel awful about what people are saying."

She brushed my comment aside. "Let them say what they want. I'm a lot tougher than I look. I was an army wife, remember?" Her smile masked the sadness that remained. "And besides, at the end of the day, even if the bill passes, it won't bring my Eduardo back. But if it doesn't, maybe hearing my story will keep other people from taking their trips unnecessarily, you know? Now that they realize this sort of thing can happen."

I nodded. I did know. It was less about winning and more about knowing you did everything you could to make a change.

"Ladies?" a staff member beckoned. "It's time."

Turner finished touching up her lipstick and took my hand. "Come on," she said. "You're going on stage with us."

Before I could object she dragged me up the steps to the stage's main level. Her name was already being announced and as supporters cheered from below, she glided behind the podium into position.

"Ladies and gentlemen, thank you for coming today to show your support for bill S.485-182, now known as 'Eduardo's Bill.' I know many of you have supported the defunding of time travel over the years and a few of you have been fighting against government sanctioned time travel since just after its inception. To you I say, our day has arrived. Based on a long-standing law banning federal funding for any program endangering an embryo, Eduardo's Bill was created by a team of dedicated men and women, some of whom share the stage with me today. In the coming days, it is up to you, the voters, to let your congressmen know you oppose time travel, you oppose government funding, and you support this bill. I hope by next week we will be living in a country which no longer finances unlawful practices and where families will live without fear of the past. Thank you all again for your support and let's pass this bill!"

Applause erupted from the crowd, and Luciana moved to take her place beside Turner as the face of 'Eduardo's Bill.' There was a touch of sadness, knowing the bill could have been named after Vicki instead, but I didn't regret my decision to keep her life a secret. As Luciana began, people called to her, pledging their support, and as I gazed out into the assembly something caught my eye. In the far-left corner was a man, standing taller than those around him, wearing a blue and orange ball cap. I squinted into the sun, trying to see his face more clearly, and that was the moment he began to wave. He leaned down to say something to the person beside him and I saw another hand waving frantically from behind the throng of constituents. Next a third hand began to wave. And then a fourth. Finally, the man looked up again and saluted.

They were all there – Lesley, Tyree, Josh, Kara… and Nate.

Overwhelmed by their presence, I bit my lower lip to hold back tears. I hadn't wanted to admit how much I missed them. How much I needed them. But seeing them out there in the crowd felt like Christmas and New Year's and my birthday all rolled up into one celebration.

I blew a kiss into the air, discreetly, and attempted to refocus on Luciana's speech, but I couldn't stop myself from glancing back in their direction.

They had no idea what I'd been through, but they came anyway.

They didn't agree with my political agenda, but they came anyway.

They were angry about being snubbed, but they came anyway.

I couldn't wait to apologize to them for my behavior and thank them for showing up. And even though I couldn't promise I wouldn't mess up again, I would try to be a better friend. I owed them that much.

The rally ended and Turner declared it an overwhelming success. There were hugs and tears and for the first time since returning from my trip, I felt as though I was finally going to be able to move forward.

I had finally forgiven myself.

As both supporters and protesters dissipated into the streets, I saw them lingering at the edge of the staging area.

The crew. My crew.

I said my goodbyes to Turner, her staff, and my team of fellow travelers, excusing myself for the evening. I approached my friends with the reverence and humility they deserved, and Nate was the first to break the awkward silence between us, scooping me into his arms.

"I'm so proud of you," he whispered in my ear.

My heart swelled.

"I can't believe you all showed up here," I stammered. "You have no idea how much it means to me."

"This bill of yours is turning out to be one of the biggest political controversies of the decade. We didn't come here for you," Josh said winking.

"Yeah," Tyree added, "we were all just like 'what should we do tonight? Let's head to DC for a rally!' Cuz we're huge activists you know."

Kara shook her head and wrapped me in her arms. "Don't listen to them. We're here because we're your friends. We don't get it, but we're here to support it."

"That's right," Lesley added. "If it's important to you, it's important to us."

"Plus, you're kind of famous and we're getting extra credit for being here," Josh said.

Nate punched him in the arm and took me by the hand. "You need a ride home?"

I shook my head. "I drove myself."

His eyes glistened, reminding me of the first time I saw them. It seemed like a million years had passed since college orientation.

"Any chance you want some company?" he asked.

We said goodbye to the others and headed in the opposite direction to where my car was parked near Turner's building. The street lights were just flickering on and headlights flashed across our path as we fell into step beside each other. I was afraid to spoil the moment by opening my mouth and so we walked without speaking until he was brave enough to break the silence.

"You just might be responsible for ending time travel," he said.

I shrugged off his attempt at a compliment. "We'll see next week," I said.

"What does the senator say? Does she think it's gonna pass?"

I didn't want to talk about the bill or time travel or Senator Turner. I wanted to talk about us.

"Maybe," I told him. "I did the best I could. Now it's up to Congress to decide."

I hesitated, considering the most delicate way to broach the subject of our estrangement. It wasn't a conversation I had ever planned on having, especially after seeing him with Erin Waters.

"I'm sorry, Nate," I said finally. "I handled this whole thing... poorly."

He chuckled, nudging me with his elbow. "You really did. But put in the same position, I probably wouldn't have handled it much better. Especially given my supposed track record."

He was referring to my story of his addiction. I wanted desperately to explain myself but was hesitant to reopen wounds that were clearly on the mend.

"I guess the reality is, we just are who we are. Regardless of what life throws our way, I deal with things my way and you deal with things your way. I'm super focused and you're completely mellow. I'm just sorry I tried to force you into being more like me. It was obnoxious to lay all that stuff on you the way I did. You didn't need to know, and I probably shouldn't have told you."

"You were just gonna hold all that stuff in forever?"

I wondered if I could have.

"I don't know. Maybe."

I showed my pass and was allowed through the gate into the parking garage. We were in the car before I worked up the courage to continue.

"I didn't tell you about my trip and Vicki because I wanted you to feel guilty. I told you because I was trying to help you understand my motivation for the bill. The choices I made were my own and none of them were your fault. I need you to know that," I told him as we merged into traffic.

He rested his hand on my knee. "I know," he said. "And I don't."

I glanced over to see if his expression mirrored the sincerity of his words.

It did.

"You were so angry though."

"No kidding," he laughed. "You're impossible sometimes."

"I'm not the only one," I said, recalling Nate in the throes of his addiction. "But you said you were done. That you couldn't deal with me anymore."

"I did, didn't I?"

"Yeah." I remembered how hard it was watching him walk away. "So why are you here?"

The lights of the city were behind us and the passing trees scattered moonlight across his face.

"I'm here because I love you," he said at last. "I've always loved you. In fact, it's the reason I stayed away all these months."

He wasn't making any sense.

"Why would you stay away if you still loved me? Why wouldn't you want to be together?"

His fingertips brushed my cheek and I rested my face into the palm of his hand.

"I did want to be together, but I would have only been in the way. You wanted to do this. You needed to do this, and I wasn't going to be the one to stop you. You obviously couldn't find a way to reconcile your heart with your head, so I decided just to take myself out of the equation."

I considered his sacrifice. After so many years, he was still surprising me, never being quite who I expected him to be.

"You're not still angry about my trip or the fact that I'm a control freak?"

"Maybe just a little," he laughed.

My voice caught in my throat. "And what about Erin?"

He cringed. "Erin Waters? Are you kidding? Is this about the other day?"

I felt like I was in middle school, vying for a boy's attention. It wasn't my finest hour.

"No," I lied.

He didn't respond.

"Yes," I admitted, slumping into my seat.

He grinned at me. "Of all the things you could be stressing about right now, that girl should be the least of your worries. She drives me crazy and follows me around like a lost puppy. She isn't who I want to be with."

"She isn't?"

"No. You're who I want to be with. I've just been biding my time."

"So why now? Why come to the rally?"

He gazed out the front window at the taillights ahead of us.

"I've been watching the news every day, tracking your bill's progress. I knew you were gone the other weekend and realized where you were when the woman with the baby showed up on TV. When I saw you after class the other day, I knew. It was written all over your face."

I couldn't believe he'd been keeping up with me the whole time, and all the while I assumed he'd simply moved on with his life.

"What was?" I asked.

"Loneliness. I let you be so you could focus on your work, but I didn't realize the toll it would take on you." He shrugged. "It was time to show up."

It was strange to think of him biding his time, watching me from the shadows. I would have never guessed he was planning to reconcile, and I could not have been more grateful. Perhaps we were destined to be together after all.

"Thanks for coming back," I said finally.

He tipped his seat back and stretched his legs as far as he could beneath the dashboard, settling in for the rest of the drive.

"I never really left," he said matter-of-factly, pulling his ball cap over his eyes. "But as long as we're getting a fresh start, I should probably thank you properly for what you did for me, using your trip and all."

I shrugged. "You don't have to thank me. That's not why I did it."

"I know," he said. "I always knew. It was just a pretty big shock when you told me. A lot to wrap my head around, you know?"

I did know. I felt like I'd spent my life recovering from one tragedy after another. I wondered if this would be the end.

"So, what's next?" he asked when I didn't respond. "When's the bill get voted on?"

"Wednesday."

"And?"

"And what?"

"And are you going to be there?"

I hadn't really thought about it. Could I handle the stress of being present when the actual decision was made, listening to each vote being read aloud to seal the fate of my hard work?

"Oh, come on!" Nate encouraged me. "You have to go. Think how amazing it's going to feel when it passes and you're a part of that history."

He was right. I needed to be there. To see my destiny through to the finish.

Chapter Thirty-Four

My phone rang Tuesday evening, and I picked up immediately when I saw who was calling.

"Hi, Charlie!" I said.

"Hey, Mel," he replied. "I just wanted to call and wish you good luck tomorrow."

I didn't know if I needed luck so much as a sedative. There was no way I was going to get a decent night's sleep.

"It's out of my hands at this point," I told him. "I wrote the best bill I knew how with the soundest constitutional argument I could come up with, and I couldn't have found a better ambassador than Luciana for the cause. If it doesn't pass it's not because I didn't try."

"It's gonna pass," he said confidently. "The news is claiming there are quite a few senators who are still undecided. That's a big deal."

"People change their minds all the time," I reminded him. "I would bet a lot of those polls are based on pure speculation."

He laughed. "Since when did you turn into such a cynic?"

"I'm working to end time travel, I think being a cynic kinda comes with the territory."

He laughed again and put Mikey on the phone to babble at me for a couple of minutes. It was funny to hear him chewing on the receiver.

"Brooke wanted me to tell you good luck from her too. She's on kennel duty tonight so she won't be back until later on or she'd tell you herself," he said after fighting to get the phone back from the baby. "We'll be watching the TV coverage tomorrow, along with everyone else in the country, so wear something nice in case the camera pans the gallery."

"You sound like Dad," I scolded him.

"Then strike that from the record," he said, "and wear whatever the heck you want!"

It was nice to be able to joke with him and it helped ease the tension for a bit. When he hung up, however, it was all I could do to keep my nerves from taking over.

That's when I heard the commotion coming from the common room of the apartment. I hesitated to open my bedroom door, but when the rhythmic bass line of my favorite song began shaking the floor, I knew I had no choice but to venture out to see what was going on.

"Surprise!" everyone cried as I stumbled into the den. In the dim light I could make out each of my friends, crowded into our tiny apartment amongst what looked to be a pretty amazing party.

Nate approached with a cup of something fruity and raised his own glass above his head. "To Melody! Today Congress, tomorrow the world!" he cheered above the music.

Everyone cried out in agreement and most everyone in attendance found their way over to wish me well and offer their support. It felt amazing to know so many people believed in me.

"You know," I said to Nate when we finally got a moment alone together in the corner of the kitchen, "you should have said 'tomorrow Congress and eventually the world' if you wanted to be more precise."

He refilled his glass from the case in the refrigerator. "I have no doubt that you'll be taking over the world before you know it," he smiled. "I just hope I'll be lucky enough to earn myself a front row seat."

I stood on my tip toes to kiss him and could taste the yeasty beer on his lips.

"I'm gonna need you," I told him. "Taking over the world can get awfully boring if you never have anyone around to remind you to have some fun along the way. In fact, maybe I can hire you on as my Personal Head of Merriment and Labor Diversion."

"I'm in as long as I can start tomorrow," he said. "I already got permission to bail on my classes since I figured you might need my help during the vote. I heard these senate things can be particularly boring."

"I've heard they can be particularly stressful," I replied, following him back to the party.

The last of our guests left just after midnight, and I ended up sleeping later than I expected the next morning. When the alarm went off at seven o'clock, it was all I could do to pry my eyes open as I dragged myself out of bed.

Despite sounding like my father, I took Charlie's suggestion to dress appropriately, wearing my most conservative business jacket and skirt. I figured if I was going to spend the day at the Capitol, I might as well look the part. At the last minute, I slipped Brooke and Charlie's lion watch onto my wrist.

I thought perhaps it would bring me luck.

"What's with the watch?" Nate asked when he noticed it on our drive into the city. "You've never worn it before."

I twisted the face around my wrist, remembering the spirit in which it was given. I would have never guessed on my eighteenth birthday that three years later I would be wearing it to a congressional vote against time travel.

"It was a present from Brooke and Charlie. It was supposed to remind me to live in the present because time only moves forward."

"After today, that might very well be the case," he said, merging onto the Washington beltway.

"I hope so," I said. "If the bill eventually passes both houses, people are just going to have to be happy with what's to come and trust that everything will turn out the way it's supposed to since there won't be an option to fix the past."

"Like you fixed my past?" he asked, raising an eyebrow in my direction.

His comment sliced at the very thin thread tying my carefully constructed principles together.

"I know," I groaned. "I'm a giant hypocrite. Every day I think about how lucky I am that I had the opportunity to save you from the pain of that addiction. And here I am, all high and mighty, about to take that ability from other people. The irony of it all isn't lost on me and some days it makes me hate myself."

"You shouldn't hate yourself, Mel. Everything would have worked out in the other timeline as well. It may have taken longer or been more upsetting, but I'm sure I would have come out of it eventually and we would have figured it out together."

I didn't know if he was only saying it to make me feel better or if he genuinely believed it was the case, but either way it was nice to hear that he didn't think I was going to be ruining other people's lives by taking away their ability to travel. I hoped that for most citizens, I would be saving them from the uncertainty of what the pulling apart and reweaving of our lives represented.

"Thanks," I said finally. "I think that too."

By the time we made it to the Capitol, the day's session was already well underway. We were escorted to the gallery and were given seats beside a crowd of other supporters whose lives had been irrevocably damaged by time travel. I waved to Luciana who sat at the far end of the row of benches we'd been assigned. Our small but mighty coalition waited impatiently together, whispering about what the senators were wearing, what a beautiful day it was, and where everyone thought was the best place for dinner – anything but the impending vote.

Half an hour before Congress was set to adjourn, the roll call vote began. I had never before seen so many senators present on the floor at one time, and as they milled around, waiting for their names to be read aloud by the clerk in alphabetical order, I thought I would burst from my seat. As the voting began, I tried keeping track of the "yeas" versus "nays" on my fingers, but my method soon proved to be ineffective. I eventually gave up trying to figure out whether the bill was going to pass and as the vote came to an end with Senators Woodson and Zimmerman, I held my breath.

And Nate took my hand.

"Whatever happens," he whispered, "your niece would have been proud to know you did your best."

I watched Senator Turner for signs that she knew the outcome. There were a few members she was unsure about, and I wondered if she'd been able to sway them in the eleventh hour. She wasn't facing me so I was relying on her body language to let me know. Unfortunately, her posture gave nothing away.

The clerk's microphone clicked on and the quiet mumblings of the floor fell into complete silence.

"Is any member of the Senate wishing to vote or change a vote? If not, the 'yeas' are forty-seven, the 'nays' are fifty-three. The bill is rejected. Mr. President?"

Cheers erupted from a sizable portion of the room and I watched Turner bow her head in defeat. We were only four people away from passing the bill on to the House of Representatives, but on this day, it was not meant to be.

Nate wrapped his arm around my shoulders and I acquiesced to the loss, resting my head on his chest. Time travel would go on and so would the associated danger. With nothing left to say or do, Nate led me solemnly out of the room.

Before we reached the stairs to the main floor, I heard my name being called from the direction of the gallery. Her distinctive accent gave her away.

"Melody, wait," Luciana called. "I have something I want to show you!"

I stopped where I was standing, and when she eventually caught up, she grabbed my arm, pulling me to the edge of the hallway.

"I'm so sorry about the bill," I said to her. "You were an amazing champion for our cause."

She turned from me, digging through the contents of her enormous purse.

"Ay," she said. "The bill was important, but maybe not the most important thing." She pulled her tablet from the depths of her bag and turned it on. "Here's what I need you to see."

She opened her email account and showed me there were over twelve thousand messages in her inbox.

"Oh no," I said. "How did people find you? Are you being harassed?"

She smiled brightly, flipping her hair from in front of her face. "Oh, there are a few crazy ones out there, but most of these messages are from people thanking me for sharing my story. Eduardo's story. They send me messages every day telling me how glad they are to know conception can be affected by time travel and that it's something to be avoided." Her eyes sparkled. "Don't you see? We might not need to ban time travel, just make sure people are aware of the threat it poses to their families. Maybe it will be enough to keep other people safe."

Before I realized what I was doing, I gathered her into my arms. "Thank you," I told her. "Thank you for doing the job I couldn't do."

She held me tightly, like the child she could no longer comfort. "It's been my pleasure," she said at last. "Keep in touch, okay?"

"I promise," I told her.

Chapter Thirty-Five

Somewhere between my bill never making it past the Senate floor, the pressure of final exams, and reconciling with Nate and the others, my life finally settled down. For the first time since Sam's life ended, throwing mine into a tailspin, I was at peace.

Luciana sent me weekly emails archiving the notes she continued to receive from thankful citizens who applauded her (and by default, us) for our courageous efforts against time travel. It was nice to know our hard work was still garnering some of the desired effect.

Senator Turner called as I was packing up to go home for the summer with news of another small victory in our effort to make the world a safer place for travelers.

"I was approached by a colleague today out of nowhere about our bill. He stopped into my office before lunch and asked if we could grab a bite to eat together before our afternoon session to discuss his proposal. Would you believe that he was so impressed by the support we gained for Eduardo's bill that he wants to spearhead his own legislation to institute mandatory changes in the traveling process based on our findings? To prevent in utero changes, he believes it should be illegal to travel during possible known conception windows for any pregnant women a traveler might come in contact with during the course of their trip."

"That's amazing," I said. "Do you think it has a shot?"

She chuckled. "Absolutely! We came so close with Eduardo's bill, Melody. The people who supported that will support this, and I have a strong feeling we opened a lot of people's eyes to this danger with our campaign." She paused and I sensed there was something more she wanted to say. She cleared her throat. "I hope you don't mind, but I mentioned that you might be willing to help out. Merely as a consultant, of course."

"I'd love to help," I told her. "Isn't that what paid interns are for?"

Nate and I headed home for summer vacation with plans to visit one another every weekend, with our annual trip to the beach thrown in for good measure. I spent my days interning for Senator Turner, assisting with the new bill and spent my evenings with Brooke, Charlie, and Mikey.

I didn't think it could happen, but I had to admit the kid was growing on me.

One especially humid evening as I sat with him on the lawn, corralling fireflies into the Mason jar on his lap and reflecting on the blessings in my life, I was struck by the simple lesson life had been trying to teach me all along. I'd had glimpses of it over the years – as a small child, after my dad's death, and skydiving with Nate, but I'd never fully embraced its truth.

Instead I'd spent all that time in a silent battle struggling against the part of myself which answered to my own addictive tendencies. And while they certainly weren't as obvious to everyone as Nate's had been, the truth was, they were there.

His addiction to hydrocodone was fueled by the need to escape the pain of his guilt over Sam's death. It was blatant. Glaring. It could not be ignored.

My addiction to control was born out of the satisfaction I took knowing I had the power to dictate the direction of my life. It was subtle and dwelled just beneath the surface of who I was. Most people didn't even realize it was there.

And although their origins were as different as their manifestations, my addiction to control was just as powerful as

Nate's addiction to pills. He lied, cheated, stole, and sacrificed friendships to get what he wanted.

And I had done the very same thing.

Like it or not, I was an addict.

Throughout my life, I'd clung to the hope that with enough hard work and sacrifice, I could achieve any goal I set my mind to. I set aside fun, the people I loved, and some of life's greatest pleasures to pursue my goals. I truly believed I could do whatever I wanted to do because I was in charge of my own destiny.

Now, in the midst of the dew soaked grass of nightfall with my nephew by my side, I was finally ready to accept that my life was out of my control. And so, in the great debate against myself over the truth of my existence, it was finally time to topple my own straw man.

Because no matter what I did or said or felt, I would never be able to control everything. I could make my own choices while I stumbled along life's path, but at the end of it all, my journey was not my own. My future, everyone's future, was in the hands of the other people who crossed our paths.

And it was also in the hands of Fate.

Life, as it turned out, wasn't about controlling that fate, but surrendering to it. About holding on to the things that were most important and letting the rest go.

"Buh," Mikey cried suddenly, holding the jar for me to see.

"What is it?" I asked.

"Buh," he said again, his smile emphasized by the two bottom teeth which had finally come in.

I stood him on my lap to ensure I had his full attention and his tiny toes dug into my thighs.

"Are you trying to tell me something?" I gasped.

He shook the jar. "Buh."

"You're saying bug, aren't you?"

"Buh!" he squealed.

I couldn't believe of all the people to hear Mikey's first word, Fate had chosen me. I scooped him up, along with his jar of glowing bugs, and held him to my chest, savoring the musky scent of little boy. I knew I'd always cherish my precious memories of Vicki, but I was learning to treasure all the other good things in my life, regardless of how they were acquired.

Things like summer nights and lightning bugs.

And Nate.

And especially Mikey.

Part Four

Spring Semester — Fourth Year

Epilogue

"Are you kidding me right now?" I called over my shoulder. "Come on already!"

Nate trailed behind me, his gown flowing like a cape behind him as he hurried to catch up.

"He's not going anywhere, you know," he said. "And you're gonna knock someone over if you don't slow down."

I had no intention of slowing down or listening to his advice. I had already missed the main event, thanks to my own graduation ceremony which my mom insisted I attend, despite my opposition. I wondered if she beat us from school to the hospital.

"I'm here to see Brooke Johnson," I told the nurse at the front desk.

She checked her computer screen. "She's a popular girl. In room one-oh-eight. Down the hall to your left and it's the third door on your right."

I thanked the nurse and powerwalked through the corridor, leaving Nate trailing behind. I could hear my family before I saw them and Mikey greeted me at the door.

"Aunt Mewady," he cried, racing across the linoleum floor into my arms.

"Hey, Kiddo!" I said, giving him a kiss on the top of his head. "I heard you have a new baby brother."

"Baby," he said, pointing to where Brooke was propped up on the bed in the center of the room, a swaddled infant tucked in her arms.

Nate joined me in the doorway and Mikey scrambled down to say hello.

"Look at you two, all dressed in your caps and gowns," Charlie commented as he strode across the room to greet us. "I can't believe out of 365 days to choose from, this little guy decided to come on your graduation. What are the chances?"

"Pretty slim," I said, giving him a hug. "I'm sorry you guys missed it, but I think having a baby there at the ceremony might have taken away from all the pomp and circumstance. And you know how universities like their pageantry."

"I do," he laughed. "And thanks for agreeing to keep your stuff on so we could see you looking like the graduates you are. Maybe we could take some pictures together outside when Mom gets here."

I rolled my eyes. Any excuse for them to pull out a camera.

I glanced at Brooke, who was flushed with the excitement and exhaustion of the day. She knew immediately what I wanted to do.

"Well come get him," she said, shifting the baby from under her bosom. "You won't believe how different he is from Mikey. They don't even look like brothers."

"What'd you decide to name him?" I asked as I approached her, arms outstretched.

A wistful look passed between Charlie and Brooke, and she smiled knowingly at her parents.

"Branson," she said. "We've decided to name him Branson."

I took my nephew gently from her arms and gazed upon the little boy who would share a name with the brother-in-law I never had the pleasure of knowing. My breath hitched in my throat and I couldn't keep myself from welling up.

"He's cute, but he's not that cute," Charlie teased. "There's really no reason to cry."

I couldn't stop myself because Brooke was right. He looked nothing like Mikey.

Instead Branson looked exactly like Vicki, with her auburn wisps and dark eyes. He was slight – not nearly the armful his brother was, and it was as if I was looking into Vicki's face and not my newborn nephew's. In that moment I knew Fate had delivered me a spectacular gift - another opportunity to be the aunt I was supposed to be to a child who would forever remind me of the value of living in the moment.

The End

Acknowledgments

First and foremost, to my fans, old and new, thank you for your continued support and encouragement. I hope that Melody's story was worth the wait.

To Anne Zirkle, for helping me to hone my craft by encouraging me with the perfect amount of eye rolling and ridiculously thorough attention to detail. Waiting for you to publish your new homonym app cuz Lord knows I could use it!

To Rick Tarr and Erin Roscoe, for giving me the inside scoop on everything UVA and Virginia Tech related. Hope I did your alma maters proud!

To my grandmother, for unapologetically pushing young adult literature to the geriatric crowd and creating a whole new fan base for me.

And finally, to my family, for putting up with the middle of the night tapping at the keyboard, the burnt dinners while I'm trying to multitask, and the inattentive stares when my mind is still writing while I'm supposed to be paying attention to you. Thank you for accepting that, like it or not, Brooke and Charlie and Melody are officially a part of our family.

Made in the USA
Columbia, SC
26 February 2018